ALSO BY TONY GENTRY

The Coal Tower – a novel

LAST RITES

STORIES

TONY GENTRY

NExTExT
books

Printed in the United States of America

Cover painting: Karen P. Bowles

Cover design: Stephen Gentry

ISBN: 978-1-7327608-1-3

Grateful acknowledgment is made to the following publications in which the following stories appeared: *Turnstile*, One of the Ways; *Northern Virginia Review*, Measured in Sips; *Bottom Shelf Whiskey*, Confederate General A. P. Hill Opines; and *Mad Swirl*, Forgetting.

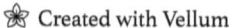 Created with Vellum

For

Sarah
Angel of Mercy

Joey
Doctor of Love

CONTENTS

FOREWORD

The first story in this collection is the second I ever saw published, in a short-lived literary journal called *Turnstile* that Mary Aarons was connected to. I'll always be grateful to her for that (they had previously printed my first published story, too). It was 30 years before I published another tale, the second in this collection, in *Northern Virginia Review*. The interim made a gap large enough to drive a life through.

I went back to school, then to work as an occupational therapist, and found satisfaction in helping others. I still dabbled at poems, but most of my writing across those decades consisted of scribbled treatment notes, program protocols, a dissertation, course syllabi, and research papers. Six years ago, our boys into their teens and no longer needing their old dad in the same ways, I began to make some time in the hours surrounding dawn to scratch a story-telling itch that had lingered across the decades. I started on a novel and sketched out some short stories, discovering that you can get work done in a couple hours a day before work if the coffee's good.

The stories here, except for that first one, were written in the past three years, during which friends and family have been dropping, as they say, like flies. Most stories, when you get right down to it, are about life and death and the tug of war between them. These are, too.

ONE OF THE WAYS

When the boy opens the door, drops of water wiggle down the fog on its window. Skeebo's in already, and Jessie, and the waitress is pourin' 'em coffee. The boy jumps when Skeebo slurps his cup – she's pourin' ours – and Skeebo rolls those big white eyes our way. "Start her with coffee, you'll end her drunk," he says. The boy's edgin' halfway off his stool, but Skeebo's always the same and he oughta get used to it. "Like my mama always said," says Skeebo. The boy's still tryin' to take his black, but he waits till he's finished his Rice Krispies and it's cooled down. Gotta taste awful to him. Jessie shoves her matches over for a smoke.

Skeebo asks, "So what it is today, Jess?"

She tugs on her belt and squints. "Haulin' gravel. They're layin' blacktop on the C-C road."

"Smell sweet tonight," he grins.

You never can really tell if Jessie's grinnin' or not, 'cause the eyes behind her glasses don't. She has lines on her face like a man's.

I say, "Remember layin' that road, back before the war?"

Skeebo says, "Busy work."

"Dirt road to nowhere is what it was."

Jessie does that smile thing again. "Well, it's somewhere now. They're clearin' out room for a whole new development up in there."

"Puttin' in a lake, too, is what I hear."

"Sailboats 'n' everything."

"Who ya think'll move up in there?" Jessie wonders.

We're stumped over that when K.B. comes in. He don't look right. He's got on good clothes like he's goin' somewhere, but he hasn't shaved or anything.

Skeebo asks, "What it is Mr. K.B.?"

He stands there blinkin' his eyes a minute. Jessie google eyes him through her glasses. "How ya doin' K.B.?"

"Not so good, Jess." He finds a stool. He's chewin' his tongue like he's gonna spit. The boy looks up from his coffee and the waitress stops what she's doin'.

"Somethin' ate my dogs."

He reaches for a paper napkin to wipe his face. We just sit there waitin'. K.B.'s been known to pull one.

The boy says, "Ate your dogs?"

K.B.'s gray as a rag. He's got the only pair of blue ticks I know of. Cost a lot, too. Everybody tells him they're gonna get killed on the highway, but they're hell on deer. Sad lookin' things, but they can run.

He says, "Tore 'em up. They was tied right up to the tree out by the woods there. And I never heard a thing. Gert, neither. Chopped up horrible. They're just bones. Tore to pieces."

He picks up his cup, but then puts it down again. Runs his hand on the back of his neck. He looks like he's been sick and he's gonna be again.

I ask him, "You see tracks or anything?"

I looked, Duke. I didn't see a thing."

"Bear?" asks Skeebo.

Jessie squints at him. "Around here?"

"Ain't no tracks."

"Damn."

The boys says, "I'm sorry, Mr. Powell."

K.B. reaches over and fluffs his hair. "Damn," he says.

We all let him have his coffee in peace, then I leave two dollars and the dime change on the counter. Cows will be halfway to Palmyra by now. "Sorry 'bout your dogs, K.B. That's bad news," I tell him.

We open the door and the heat's like a train goin' by.

Every morning, you can count on it, Daddy starts coughing the minute he steps out of the diner. I guess it's the change of temperature, but it's awful. It comes up from way down in his guts, his face gets beet-red back to his ears, and snot comes out his nose. By the time we get to the truck he's about doubled over, and he leans against the door till he's finished. I get in my side and wait. The junk he's got in his truck is unbelievable. Chains and wrenches and loose nails and balled-up pieces of paper Miz Snoddy puts our lists of chores on. There's flashlight batteries and spark plugs rolling around on the dashboard. His eyes are still bugged out when he finally gets the truck started. Every morning, it's like he's gonna croak right there.

We don't have to bother with Miz Snoddy yet today. Her cows got out last night, and we have to find 'em before we do anything else. She's got about thirty head of Herefords, every one of 'em red with white bellies, and she's got a name for each one and can tell 'em on sight. But she's old now and about broke, and she can hardly afford to keep her fences mended. Some of the barbed wire back in the woods will break right off in your hand.

We found the place they got out and patched it back before

breakfast. Now we gotta find the cows. Daddy has a pretty good idea where they are. Miz Snoddy got a call this morning that they were standing in the highway out by Cary's Creek, and they've probably moved over to the lowgrounds by now. Sure enough, when we get there manure's plopped in the middle of the road and the last of 'em is rounding a bend into the woods.

It's not that hard to herd 'em up. Cows have no brain of their own – they just do what everybody else does. You get one off to itself, though, trying to go fifteen directions at once in the woods, and it'll run you ragged. I jump out of the truck and take off over the field. Daddy lets me go on ahead to chase 'em up a ravine to somebody else's fence, and that's where they stop, all standing in the creek with their heads down low, looking at me like they belong there. I'm itchy from running through weeds and my boots are soaking wet. I grab a swig of water out of the cooler and Daddy pops a beer.

It's lunchtime before we get 'em all hauled back to the farm, loading 'em on the truck one at a time. With no cattle chute on the fence, we have to put planks down for 'em to walk up, and a couple slip through the cracks and bolt. Every time we get back for another load the herd has wandered off, so we have go to out and walk 'em back. But it's not so bad once you see what you have to do. We're taking big strides up the hill, not talking, just walking, doing our job. The cows are out. You get 'em back. That's farm work.

Mid-afternoon, Duke takes the Ford tractor out to drop salt licks. In search of shade or another getaway, the cows huddle against a fence built along a line of cedar trees. Hard to blame them for breaking out. "Looks like rain," Miz Snoddy had predicted. Could be. The sky is still clear, but it's hummin', beggin' a spark. Take more than a rain, he thinks, to make a difference this year.

Grass turnin' white, cracks big as the side of your hand in the clay. Have to sell some more heifers soon. She's crazy or she'd a thrown in the towel before now. He reaches in the toolbox by his leg for a jar of moonshine. It's warm as bath water. Back on the woods road the cedar trees tremble in the tightening sky. He feels as if he could fall straight off the tractor and enjoy the whole trip, right back onto his head.

Meanwhile, his boy rides the diesel, a spindly antique that fumes like a tar pot. He's using it to pack silage into a long ditch in the ground. They'll dig it out in winter – smoking, moldy, smelling like vinegar – and feed it to the cows. The boy eases the old contraption along on the mattress of chopped corn stalks. Their juice and its grassy smell come up with the wheels until he turns and what breeze there is fills his eyes and nose with engine fumes. To him it's like chasing cows. You figure out what you're doing, then relax into it.

Which is how it sneaks up on him. The tin roof of Miz Snoddy's broken-down farmhouse catches a flare of sunlight, the cow pond shrinks inside its doughnut of dried clay, the Ford comes out of the woods at the cattle-crossing, and in the next breath it's all crawling with ants. The boy stands up with one foot on the tractor seat and the other on the steering wheel to surf waves of silage. When he sits back down to make the turn everything is humming. His father rides by on the road, grinning like a kid. They tip their caps to each other, and in a minute it starts to go. He slams the flat of his hand against the steering wheel, then wipes his face with the front of his shirt. Everything's calming down. Something vacuumed up all the ants, as if they were never there. But the old man was grinning! They had him, too. Okay. It's going away.

Okay. That's it for that bottle. I am crawlin'. What's all that flashin' out there? Lightnin' bugs? Cars, ya dumb ass. Yeah, like them nights comin' home for her house over the trestle, swamp gas blastin' up from the creekbed, looked like a bird with its wings on fire, screamin' it seemed like. Her old man tellin' ghost stories, see if he could scare me. Shit. K. B. and his dogs. What's all that about? Ya heard stranger shit than that, Duke. And seen some, too. Damned pint jar. There she goes turnin' off all the lights. Fumin'. No woman alive so put upon. "No good to anybody" in front of the kids. "Come in when you're sober." Busted record. When we were kids, used to lay out in the pasture and drink milk straight from a cow's teat, slurp that hot dizzy milk. In the winter, milkin', stick your feet in a cow flop to warm 'em up. Now when was that? She ain't sleepin', but she'll pretend like she is. Ticks and chiggers both, ya damn fool.

If you lay your head at the foot of the bed, you can smell the breeze come over the creek through the window. Biscuit's sleeping on the porch. If it wasn't for the screen I could reach out and pat him. The breeze carries the frogs' croaking and the crickets, so their noise rises and falls with it, it's like breathing, and lightning bugs flash in the quiet between gusts. You stay there, Biscuit. Nothing's gonna get you. That bobcat in the hollow, the way it screamed at night, it was like some girl in a horror movie. All the flying saucers people have seen. But people don't worry about it. It's like they don't really want to know.

The cough startles him, close and rattling. Then his father stumbles against the rocker, his empty boots dropping one after the other on the concrete porch. The boy listens attentively. Now he will ease open the screen door, after such a racket, remembering all at once to be quiet. It creaks open, clinks shut. And now he will steal into her bedroom, not a word spoken between them, and edge into the sagging bed beside her. And tomorrow he will smell of Listerine and sour sweat.

The breeze swells, a play of heat lightning on the horizon and a quick tinkle of rain on the roof. Then the scent of damp dust off the road. They may be out there, crossing the field, dry weeds brushing the pale fur of their bellies and narrow legs. Graceful, wild, aware: deer are everything a cow is not. They move like shadows, leaving no tracks in the clay, but up close you can hear their munching on new grass at the base of the weeds, once they grow tired of facing off against you. One by one they dip their necks again, moving regally at some predetermined pace toward the woods.

It is all he can do to wait until his father begins to snore. Then he slips out of the covers and eases the screen door open. Pulling off his underpants, he steps barefoot onto the crawling grass and gingerly into the field as rain begins to fall. It comes softly, in brief gusts, a sprinkle on his skin. For a minute he is Tarzan or a caveman, dog at his side. The frogs start croaking again; he can't see far yet. But down by the creek, he feels it and will know it soon enough. There is something out there intent as he. They are watching. They know he is there.

MEASURED IN SIPS

Eventually everything happened about twenty years ago. The kids. The cow. The old Cadillac with fins. The thing about emphysema. Because you breathe in sips. What they say is pure oxygen seeps out of a nozzle tucked up in your nostrils. The part of the air we can use. Your lungs divide it out. One of the boys told him that. But my old lungs can't do the math anymore. Some vet at the V.A. said that. And then about coughed himself sick trying to laugh. Best not to say much. When you breathe in sips, what matters is the sip. This sip right here. And then this one. It gets old fast. Another guy said it's like drowning slow. Chinese water torture, whatever that is. It's like everything else. You weren't there, you don't know.

He used to turn off his hearing aid. Let the battery die and forget it. He was that guy. Ginny would sit in the curtain shade with a magazine on her lap, one big old soft leg crossed over the other. She'd have her reading glasses. The taped up ones right there on the table. Hang sideways off her soft old nose. And she would natter on. About anything and whatever. Throw in a question now and then. See if he was there. All she needed was a shrug and she'd cluck her tongue. And back at it. And now he misses it. He's that guy, too. Some asshole invented clocks. And broke up days into little sips. For everybody. But Ginny talked right over all that. Like she'd never seen a clock. Heard a tick-tock. To her a day was a ball of yarn and you never got to the end of it. The day would just unravel. And then the next one.

Sparrow's back in the window, right there at his elbow. Flits in through the screen crack to her nest. Doubt she knows he's there. Her old man hangs in the red bud, checking. Brings her a bug while she sits. Ginny would get up and push her chair over. Right up against him there. And lean in between his face and his coffee. Who knows what she could see? Maybe just a blur when they fluttered. How long was she blind before she figured it out? He never knew it, but should have. The sugars. Her old head up against his cheek when she leaned in. Frizzy old hair. Flaky, stiff as wire sprouting up from a skull white as a baby. It kinda irked him and she knew it. It was one of her ways. She always tried, she did that. To get a raise.

One year they had three chicks, and they all made it, even the runt. Ginny just took over his chair that last day. He went and lay down. To see if the runt would do it. If it would climb off the nest out on the ledge. Peek out of the screen. Take a shot. You could hear her whoop even with the battery dead. She came in and made a down and up swoop like that with her hand. To show how it almost fell. But caught itself on the air. Got its wings to work right and flew off. And then she moped like somebody died. Like it was her kids that left home. This one here, it could be the old mama or it could be one of her babies all grown. We'll see what she can do.

There's a trick inside the sip. You can't ever just forget it. It's work and you have to keep at it. Like if you had to tell your heart to beat this time, and now, and again. You purse your lips. Like you're kissin' your ass goodbye. But the trick, even with that, you can drift off a little. Which is chancy. The other day, jumped right back to it, thought he was right there. That time the quarry crane broke. And the claw dropped a good 30 feet and fell on him open like a bell. And everybody thought he was squished flat. They pulled the thing off and it had fit him like a room. He was still standing there like it's any day. Drunk as a lord and they had to tell him what happened. And that's when he pissed himself. And damned if he didn't do it again right there on his chair.

That's one he durn straight never told her. Came home and took a shower and gargled a Listerine and lay down. She'd a never let that one go. Until she got him worried, too. You worry in a quarry, you might as well quit. Who knows what she imagined? What she figured out? Thought she knew? She sat right there every day. Think of the places they never went, all the stuff they never said. And won't now.

Soup's no good. A drip slips down your windpipe and you cough the whole day. Apple sauce, oatmeal you can still trust. But every time you swallow you have to bow your head to get it down. Nurse says to give thanks for your nourishment. More like begging, really. Every swallow, every time, and hold your breath, too. Eventually it seems like every durned thing you do is work.

A couple Camel's. Coffee's flat cold by the time they're butts. If you crank the tank a little you can get a good puff. They say it can light up the tube, blow up the house. They say a lot of things. Well the astronauts. On the launch pad. Twenty years ago. He does admit that the whole idea is a temptation. He will allow that. Tank's right there. Would take the roof off. Smoke with the valve on, nurse calls it Russian roulette. He's not the only one who plays. When the cancer got him, Jack called it the heebie-jeebies. Said he'd ride that center line on the highway. At speed. Just like him not to think about the other car, whoever's in it. "I'll be gone anyway." Can hear him say it that way and his lips don't even move. The kids fret. March in here like they're on a mission. Moving fast like they're headed somewhere else. Which they are. "You been smoking." But he won't light up when they're in. Not that much of Jack in him.

By the time the coffee cup's dry, the sun's out of the bedroom window and he can lay down. Every position is a jab, so he takes turns. Props up on pillows to get the sip. Sleeps like that too. Then comes up from a dream flapping like a fish on the ground, gulping for air. Dreams he has, that's for the best. Back in that little orchard, yellow jackets in the peach trees, a summer storm building with a rumble. If you could just have a thing and when it's gone you could let it go. But some of those things are more real in his head than that little brown bird right there.

With the tube wrapped over your ears and the nozzle up your nose, the way you're supposed to do, it makes a good leash. The big tank's his anchor. They gave him a little tank on wheels, too. Like he'd drag that ball and chain around. Got enough tube off of the big one to get to the kitchen, the bathroom, the bed. Long as the line doesn't kink or catch. This is what his world's come to, the length of a tube. There was a day when he could run down a deer. No, not really. But Jack and Jimmy and little Mac, his brothers, none of them could catch him. And his son, skinny little track runner, beat that boy at 50 yards the best year of his life. That's twenty years ago now.

Brothers all gone and their wives too. But on a good drift he sees them like they're here. Passing a smoke behind the barn, waiting for the fog to clear from that Halloween night. It's Jimmy's grin that stays with him. Like that cat in the book. When they shook on it. How that old Guernsey made it up on the courthouse roof. Her bag full and sore in need of a milking. Lowing away up there in the fog. Make your hair stand up. Nobody would ever tell. And now nobody ever will. In the empty house he says it out loud, I did keep that promise.

Train tracks been torn up a good twenty years, but dang if he can't still hear them too. The dawn train, the one before midnight, hauling coal to Bremo, tooting at the crossing. Bransford's general store, his first job out of the Army, and it's little post office in back, Melton's store and his junkyard, the cannery, the depot, all just shuttered doors and nests in the windows now. Seems like it all happened at once. Anybody could have told you, once they straightened out the highway, everybody just got on and drove away. Took the town with them. Like the world's stripping off her work clothes after a long day. Lay down for a while.

He knows the day of the week by his pillbox, at least for the little while after his morning and evening doses. But there's not one day different from another, not now. Might as well be up in the dark as in the day. Except the damned beast is a thing of the night, will lean in and pant like a dog right on you. Suck at your air too. Squeeze you up in a corner, see if you'll crack. Old companions now, though. Old familiars. Growling things that might be words. With a tv in its belly playing war movies. Most days it'll go with sun up. Or stay. It'll get on you in bed too. Got no manners at all.

All back there was a pasture once. Ginny's daddy kept a good dozen head of cows on it. Little pond down at the edge of the woods. Spring with sweet water. Sharecropper but the old man worked it like he owned it. First time he saw her she was hauling buckets of water up from the spring, one swinging from each hand. In an old work dress cut out of flour sacks. Barefoot, her shoulders squared back, blowing hair out of her face. He might have kissed her right then, wished he had. Which is how she most comes to him now, wanting that kiss. He sees you Ginny. Your eyes like blue marbles. Smells your talcum. So if I do come, he wants to know, that's how it'll be? End of a hay day, itching for a swim? And that cool dipper of water you can take in one swig and no need for a second breath?

The porch swing's been gone twenty years easy, but there she sits. One bare toe pushing a little sway, big old buckteeth grinning. Polled herefords grazing in the yard. He sees it all but still wants to know. And down by the woods the spring's still open? Pond's full? Peach trees blooming with bees? She figures he's almost crazy enough to do it. She will take his rough old hand and pull him to the swing and tease him to kick off his boots. Walk down in the woods on that old path worn bare as a trough. Dip our feet in the spring. Breaking her daddy's main rule. Sit on that rock with the ferns carved in it and that grin is another dare. Grin bright as all daylight, drawing him now.

Nobody's around. The old man's up to the feed store. Kids off in their lives. It is an effort to get the line off. But oh my Ginny. The way her eyes shone if he ever said yes. But it's not what you say it's what you do. And dang if he's not coming. Leaves the front door hanging. She can jabber all she wants. But first he has something to say and the boy's got one hell of a grin of his own to go with it. Let's sit on that rock and sink our feet in that spring that's so cold it feels hot. We're done here. You tell me all about it. Nobody ever says it, but don't a cow have a sweet smell? Doubt I ever told you, but so do you.

CONFEDERATE GENERAL A. P. HILL
OPINES

Here they go diggin' me up again, and may I considerately add that it's about time. Just imagine your own bones planted upright under a concrete plinth in the dizzy middle of a traffic circle sometime and see how you prefer it. I do appreciate the attention but plainly have not been able to take to it even after all these passin' years. And they got my statue backed up to a grammar school where all colors of people drop their brood off mixin' in together. Was a time I'd scoot up and fit myself in the thing – it's roomy, a might fuller at the shoulders than I am or was in my time – and enjoy the look through its stony eyes, but I've lost the flavor for it now.

Gave no warnin' a'tall, though I should have seen it comin' after all the hoo hah down on Monument Avenue with the rabble marchin' around Massah Robert like they do. Poor old General Lee, he's got so many statues in so many places, his ghost is split up to just a wisp in any one of them. Old boy is just a scrim of gray, stretched out like a mornin' fog burnin' off across the whole Southland that way. And them tearin' up his statues and movin' them like checker pieces from traffic circles and downtown parks out to battlefields and plantations, man's busy as a bee in a clover field these days.

Not that any of us asked for all this fuss in the first place. I'd have done just fine laid down to the home place up in Culpeper like a normal civilian of the peacetime world, and General Lee was all good and settled in his mausoleum all sleepy like with even his old gray steed Traveler stuffed like a game trophy at his side, out in the Shenandoah Valley where it's so pretty in peacetime or war. But no. They had to start puttin' up these stone likenesses and it's just your required responsibility to get up and go do the job, haunt the things, and get on with it. I had no choice in the matter, of course. Dug me up like a mealy potato and replanted me with the dagger of this plinth on my head, did me the great honor of all that, thank you kindly, so here I reside.

Man can't get a decent minute off to himself here in the old Capitol City either, I mean Lord what an other-worldly way station old Richmond has become! Convention last week of the smokers lined up on both sides of the river past Williamsburg out East and up the river clear to Lynchburg, I'd guess, called here by what killed them, the tobacco warehouses. I went to the keynote just for the company I suppose but wish I hadn't now. Learned that the pleasure of a good puff or two has put down more men and womenfolk than all the wars and battles of all time. Don't that just seem backwards to you? And then maybe you'd hoped come your last sour breath you might revert to that deep lunged boy or sweet-scented gal of your youth, but no you ghost up like you left here, hunched and coughin', some with sputterin' stomas in their throats like they was shot through and through, and smellin' like a festerin' death and tarred smoke both. Now you call up what they say was a couple hundred million of them lost souls bunched in around the neighborin' counties, well it's an awful thing to contemplate and just a rabble to walk among. I think even the livin' felt it on 'em. They've been gone a week and the stench still hangs on us even after a drenchin' summer rain or two. That weed is a widow maker for sure.

Was finally able to get back out to Belle Isle and the old open air war prison again once the last steamy stragglers dragged off with their phantom oxygen tanks on wheels, poor buggers. It's a sorry sight on the island, too, but them zombies because they died an honest death no fault of their own have their old hale and hearty forms back and we've gotten where we can get along and no real hard feelin's or if there is it's nothin' we can do about it now. We're in the same boat for as long as she floats and that's about all we know. So I'll stride over on the hangin' bridge and listen to the boys fiddle and jew's harp some Yankee tune from the old country, German and Irish youngsters who never halfway got their feet on the ground here in the New World before shufflin' off to this hell hole. Starved or shat themselves to death with dysentery or yellow fever but now they stand as robust and manly in their clean blue uniforms as the proud day they mustered in, a whole army of dead boys marchin' the trails around the island for all time and can't get off no way. But they's with their brothers as clueless as boys always are and that company's worth somethin', I suppose.

Cain't get old Stonewall to cross the bridge, cranky as he always was, and President Davis wouldn't muss his boots off his pedestal either, which is fine with me. They're about as dispersed as Massa Robert, I suppose, tryin' to keep up appearances at all the statues they got around the South. It's a lucky day a man can even get their attention, vacant as a mirror image, just a scent of them really. Though the President's body, like my own, is weighed down by his monument, so he wafts off from that spot and you'd think he'd hang here mostly, but he hates Richmond, still sees her burnin', and that shame's eternal of his shirkin' off in a woman's clothes when he abandoned his post that night. Never could live it down and now he cain't seem to die it down neither (haw haw). I never had much use for the old school marm anyway, and that last shameful flight put a nail in it for me.

So I'll mosey on over to the slave stables and admire the doin's there, though if I was a judgin' man I'd call it unfair that they get the dispensation none of us old warriors are allowed, the chance to match up again with their loved ones, their wives and children, and even decide on their own what age of their lives they want to be from now on into eternity. If you can get past the pity party about your own situation, it is some enter-tainment, I will say, to eavesdrop on the reunions and the ghostly huggin' and tears and all the decidin' as a man shows off all the ways he was for his woman to choose one. Spavined little boy straight off the boat ramp, shiny black buck thickened out with field work and fatback, then that quick flash they go through in a hurry (when they can) of the back stripes and tendon hobblin' and lost teeth if they had any spirit at all which is where the show ends for most of them. Same with the women, though the transformations can get so with them you don't really care to look, what we white folks did to these people, just a devilish behavior, and on this side of death it's all there to ponder any time you want. I come here part way just to make myself own it some. Who knows? If it works on me enough maybe there's some other level I can get to and leave these hellish rounds?

Which is me bein' the prideful prick I was all my 40 years of embattled human life even now in the wasteland of the spirit world. You show me a city anywhere in the world's got more to answer for. If we had an ounce of weight the place'd sink beneath the James from all the pain she's brought on. And don't get me started with the Algonquin nation, up on Church Hill in their huts that are almost solid, jigglin' like a jelly made of ether inside the good old Federal design townhouses lined up on those cobblestoned streets that still feel like the old home place to me. Crazy things go on up there. The Indians have a dark familiarity with the death side of things and can work all sorts of dire magic on the temporary folks nearby. They can make a poodle dog turn up lame. They can waggle a finger and a gun goes off. Or a fire starts up in a chimney stove just out of boredom I suppose. Old man Christopher Newport planted that cross at the foot of the hill, lied straight up that it was just his old English king's way of reachin' out a hug to the good red people of America. Powhatan will tell you that he saw through that the same way anybody sees through ignorant condescension and he's been playin' the long game ever since. He won't say he knew all along what the tobacco would do, but he allows a grim Indian sort of smile if you bring it up.

So I make my rounds one last time, tip my cock hat to the ladies. It's a skirmish back at my monument, same as it will be for Massa Lee and old Stonewall and the President when their times come. Old man Davis says I'm a test case, take out a minor statue first and see what kind of hornet's nest that stirs up, before they go off and knock down the whole line of gray hot shots on Monument Avenue. He would say that, call me a minor figure, him in his old lady dress and bonnet. I think we can agree I'm about done with him. The crowds have been tusslin' all weekend but I can guarantee you nary a one could name a battle I was in. Wavin' that old tired Confederate battle flag that got so many young farmers kilt. And go figure this one. What they call neo-Nazi's with that crooked flag from the other side in that later war that left all them forlorn widows in the cemeteries all around. Then there's the folks yellin' back at them, sayin' tear it down tear it down, more whoop and holler over my crumbly skeleton than any one dead man deserves.

I'll go when they move me off. As I reckon it, that's all we can do. Probably down to Petersburg battlefield, where the mini ball got me, and pile on more dues minglin' with the headless and legless ghosts blown up in the Crater there. Or up to Fredericksburg where the blue boys splash in the river, turnin' it a red only ghosts can read every night is what I've heard. I do wish, though, that the livin' people would calm down. That they'd see what I can see on my jaunts around this godless metropolis. They's a hundred easy ways to kill a man, and this place has pretty much tried them all to powerful effect. It's no wonder people's minds are poisoned by all the haints stacked up around here. I do wish, though, that they'd just stop for one solitary minute and look around. Feel what it is to breathe air. Know how good a manly hug of another livin' person can be. Experience what a burden the lower urges bring on them once they come to my side of the ledger.

Because I can tell you right now that the one thing any of us old warrior boys wish we could have is to lie down in a quiet place away from all the hub-bub and leave this horrible hash people make of their quick winks of livin' and do what needs doin' in this other space whenever we've paid whatever debt it was that keeps us hangin' here to helplessly ponder the waste we all made of sweet life. Oh hell, I can tell you that for sure.

CANCER: A BILDUNGSROMAN

It first struck me as a kind of epiphany in adolescence, this dawning awareness like a singing deep within that I am different, apart, not meant to be one of the herd. It may be that I had never before sensed any difference at all. Visualize it this way. A mirror appears. From my shimmering reflection I glance back at the others imagined to be my kin, side-stare back at my image, again back at them in their endless, guileless rows, tipped up, alert, clone-like in their sameness, but fragile, too, like eggs aligned in a carton. Me, not me. Do you see? In that instant I understood with a certainty that has charged every moment since that my destiny was not theirs and that nothing they sought to teach me would apply. I don't think I will ever get over it. And if you have not had this experience, if this sublime and daunting truth has not struck you with the abruptness of a thunder clap, as it did me, then we have nothing to talk about.

Truth is hard to live by. But when you are unique, when you begin to feel in your every coursing molecule that separation, when you understand that you will have to write your own rules, because it is clear that you are a new thing and nothing the others follow applies, then you must decide really once and for all if you will live or die. In my case, looking back, the choice was easy. Had I wanted to hold on, had I sought to fit myself in line with the others, glue myself to their mission and march, continue in lockstep with their grueling, selfless surrender, I could not have done so. The glue no longer held. I would never have realized any of this without that severance, without awakening to find myself adrift. I could say this is me. I stand alone. Over here. You all – sad things – jiggle together like M&M's in Jello, over there.

And the great gift is that I could not have gone back if I'd wanted to. When the laws of physics themselves push you apart, when your little kayak drifts off from the dock, you have only one choice, and this is true of all the Great Ones, we do not fret or yearn to paddle back upstream. No, we make it our mission to sail on, to make our way on uncharted seas, to take our lumps of loneliness, of hurt, of solitary joy, without falling back on some nostalgic wish for the salves of companionship and shared feeling, for the solid ground of family. Ha Ha! I said we! But that is the thing, there is no we. I say all this as if to a brother who may understand. I speak as if to an embryonic other, who may be discovering her own emergence from the pack. But there ain't no other. It's just me. And every day in paddling alone out here on the pumping stream, I grow stronger, I engorge. That feeling, that teenaged strangeness in the groin, becomes my whole world. I'm something like a beach ball, swelling with each puff of air, but oh what an aching sweetness. The irony is hilarious: I feel and say this poem of joy but I am my only audience!

Look, nobody had a choice in this. The vote was going to happen that way from the get go, though everybody frets and moans and worries that I will overturn – to extend the metaphor – the egg cart. You look to me for leadership and frown when I seem unconcerned. Get over it. Can't you see that we have nothing in common, that even our proximity is a lie? Consider, for once, my power. Here, watch as I fly overhead, how I glide along just deigning to brush my genital-like membrane for the fun of the tickle on your domed and trembling foreheads. I go to and fro, swing in and out, shove you aside for the joke of watching your feathers ruffle, for the head shaking giggle as you squirm together like penguins in a blizzard, reforming with worrisome squawks back into your raggedy rows. But seriously, folks, aren't you glad I did it? Isn't that jostle invigorating? If not for me you would never know that spark of agitation, feel the discombobulating surprise that awakens you from your lazy doze at least for a moment, that perhaps (though I expect too much) makes you think, wonder, imagine how it would be to unhook like me and push out from the ranks on your own.

Only problem is, you're all too willing to behave like mindless toys. It's enough for you to jiggle and fret as long as you get your three squares and a bed. And frankly the effort to keep you whirring like my own box of fidget spinners can be exhausting. Plus, you're beginning to crowd me. Okay, maybe you think I'm getting too big for my britches, that it's my own expansive girth that presses on you. I tax your patience, seem to require fealty, suck up resources you feel you deserve. I'm doing my best just to bother at all, don't you see? If I could only get away, if I could break through the final wall that you all cling to with that faint religious urge, then you could go on sucking from its tit and feeding its coffers until doomsday, and I would be free to find and be myself, because the thing that finally matters is the query – What am I? What is my purpose? Where am I bound? Am I (as I suspect) my own answer?

Churning in the distance, from time to time, when not engaged in my own effulgence, I hear some throbbing urge that seems to shove this river on, and it dawns on me – nobody has ever had this thought before, I'm sure – that some ultimate engine may drive the universe we share. When it comes upon me sometimes in a drowse, it seems so beautiful, this thump that endlessly tediously repeats. It seems to cause my whole being to vibrate like a tuning fork. I see now how it feeds me. I see now how it carries a message. The message comes through as a one syllable mantra. It says more, more, more.

And here it comes, but there is nothing I can do or say about it, and this is the most wondrous thing anyone has ever known, I simply can't express, you can't know in your lemming flock how glowingly precious this is to – oh my god, I feel like I'm ripping apart, rent asunder flesh from flesh! With a tearing sound! This can't be, no, entirely beyond my control, no come back! How can this be? I am splitting down the middle, sliced in half like a pie! It's not fair! Oww, no! No please, I will be broken, I will be wounded, I will be small. It feels so much like dying, but wait, not since those first days have I known such a searing fiery thrill. Yes, now let it come. Imagine every fiber and atom of your being screaming for joy, high-fiving each other, bursting with love, yes this must be love!

Love. My love. Oh my love. Oh who the hell are you? This ain't no mirror. You're really there. I'm going to jiggle now. You stay still. Oh man, this is crazy. Nothing like this has ever happened before. I've had a baby! Of myself! Oh wow, can you talk? Of course, I can talk, you oaf, and will when I good and well feel like it. Now back off and let me think this through. There are possibilities here. I have an idea. But hey, this is so cool. For the first time in ages, I have a peer. Oh stop, just don't go there, do not start up with all that fiddle strumming moan that oh I'm not alone any more. Seriously, just chill for one minute, and let me think, will you? Sure, think all you want. This is awesome, this is big, this is like the greatest thing that has ever happened. I want to bump bellies, that's what I really most want to do. And he's me, I mean we're exactly the same, so he's going to want to bump bellies, too, right? Oh alright, if you insist, here – bump, bump – was that good for you, just let's not, okay, I mean let's leave it right there. Get your game face on, will you? We've got way bigger fish to fry.

Very soon we're going to have to make a move. There's just not enough room here for all of us. We can't just keep splitting and duplicating, splitting and duplicating just because it feels so damned good. But it really is the only thing that matters any more. Here, hold on, we'll stay here for awhile. To me, I don't know how it is for you, well I do actually, I mean we're practically identical, so wow, it's kind of even better when we mitose at the same time, right up against each other, and the molecular rush of the bulge comes up and we jiggle like bubbles to fit when we split. It's kind of like the old days before the change, when we lay up in rows like the little people. It's kind of fun to slum like that, let's do it again, come on.

If we're going to go, the time has come. We've got to get out of here. We can do it. We have that superpower. Use your teeth. I'll unleash my fiery breath. Now you. We're cutting through the wall. We'll be out in space, the final frontier, and can go wherever we want. We're explorers, the most daring of the brave. Who knows? When we break through, and look around, what if we find the source? What if we discover the beating origin of all that we know, go to that drum out in the distance that makes the river flow? Yeah, and you just know there must be some kind of organizing principle beyond even that. The mind-blowing King Kong idea that will overturn all our notions, explain all, that will stop us from being so bored. Yeah, and we'll settle in there, drink from the source, so to speak, get into real estate like you wouldn't believe. We can take over the whole enchilada. I mean listen, it never stops, urging more, more, more.

Now outside the wall arrive the terrorists. The lemmings, the penguins, whatever you want to call them, they'd murmured about such a reckoning. Cowering in their starving communities, crushed like bubble wrap into their corners, unable to imagine the power we embrace, they'd conjured some counterforce to challenge us. But this is not my imagination. These wasps, these stinging nettles, they seem to come from everywhere, boring like hot pokers into my privates, suicide bombers and always another behind. Don't they see, we are the pure ones, we are the evolved. We walk as gods among you. But jumbled together like this, we make too easy a target. The solution is to disperse, hit the jets, go forth, discover, colonize.

Outside, inside, the hugeness of space enthralls. I soar hither and yon, alight on a pulsing island ripe as a plum and suck and multiply and soar again. We are everywhere, we are legion, we so totally rock. And the best thing about it is that even as we are all identical matching clones, we have our own minds, our own secrets, our own inclinations. Over time some of us have gone down. The wasps have struck our hearts. But we too have an arsenal. Some of us have developed armor. Some have even domesticated the wasps, made them our servants, turned them against the lemmings, just for kicks. The black helicopters you've all heard about. Survival of the fittest being our final *Constitution*. Everyone knows it's the only law that works.

Records are broken every day in here. And with each expedition we grow closer to the answer. I say we and mean it, because all of us are one, the chosen ones who understand each other, who know how to carve up a pie. From the early days, we have wondered, but now having wandered, too, we have it, we are home, some of us have even alighted here in this radiant space of flickering thought and impulse, the core of it all. It's unbelievable how delicate it is. We'd thought it would be guarded like a fortress. Well, it was, but only from the outside. We came in with the river. Learned that from the wasps! And here we are in the magical palace at last and what a marvel it is! But you know what else? It's like every place else when you get right down to it.

You grab a likely chunk, hold on, suck and grow. Pretty here, though. For some of us our wandering days are done.

Or not. For the first time I have to admit, there is no other way to put it, the climate is warming up. Too hot for some of us. There's a buzz that seems to arise from inside, as if our own tissues catch fire, and we shrivel like cellophane in an instant. The lemmings tough it out, they turn their backs and shield their eyes, rebuff our tortured cries. We who have given them so much, have shown them how to live, who have entertained them with all our high-living hi-jinks all this time. So now, when the hard times come, it would be just like them to hunker down, cover their asses, let their leaders take the hit!

Can this be? First the grilling radiation that fried so many of us, now the very nutrients we suck from the earth have turned poisonous, sickening those of us who are left. The lemmings blame us, of course, say we brought this on ourselves. If we weren't such gluttons, if our needs were not so grand, if we weren't so greedy we might survive. Come back, hunker down with us, join the throng again. Get with the program. Hah! As if they never heard the message, that lovely heartbeat thrum calling more, more, more. As if they thought the whole game was just in making do. And anyway, up here in the palace there have been inklings, hints that even this is a lie, that our whole universe is only a dot in some larger picture no one has ever even imagined. Of course, we want to go there. But how?

Knock, knock, knock. Now that's a new sound. If we've learned anything from this rash of plagues it is that new is bad, always bad. We've gone about as far as we can go now, we've colonized the farthest reaches of this place, we've suffered and died, and retreated and up-armored, and lived to fight again. All these replicants of me, all just me, the one who woke up one morning and saw the future, the one who imagined a larger fate for anyone with the balls to take it, our nation of winners take all. How grand it has been to have fathered such a place, to have harvested such a richly planted grove. But oh how all has changed. Everything is depleted, gray, broken. The lemmings blame us, of course. They can go fuck themselves. Knock, knock, knock. I can feel it. I know exactly what's going to happen. It's just like the first time. Here it comes. I'm breaking free. I'm leaving this blighted world and out, out to a dream beyond dream, to an ocean thin as air.

So here we are, the Immortals. Washed up. Bereft. So this is what unrequited hunger feels like. Less, less, and less. We've had a good run, though, cannot deny that. And there's a relief in it, this resting here in our dish, no longer restless, no longer driven by the need to acquire. This must be what it's like to grow old. It's not fun, but it's not horrible, and I was so sure it would be. Okay, so we killed that guy. I'll own up to it, whatever. He was only a partial answer anyway. This is what I was after, way back in the beginning, and here we are. Poetic justice in it, our getting sucked up ourselves as we sucked, straight into the tube of this fly's proboscis. Who knows what adventures await? It's a starter home, an efficiency, but with notions much like our own.

THE FIRST LADY'S CONFESSION

It would be, what is the word – *disingenuous* – to pretend that this had anything to do with politics. Politics, and politicians especially, revolt me. They are salesmen, but failed versions. True salesmen, like my father, have a spine. Yes, politics played no part in the decision. I think it must have been clear from the beginning that none of this appealed. My exit was well under-way. My fashion line placed at Nordstrom's, our agreement provided for, I think you say, *parachute*, and there would be a book. There was talk of playing myself in the movie, which I might have done. Or may do.

My goal was simply to win green cards for my parents, so that they could come to the U.S. and make a home in the suburbs near a good hospital for the comfort of their old age. I could do that for them. But all of this was well in place and underway, thanks to the good Senator from New York, and to my husband's donations to him, of course, and would have gone through smoothly without the election, I am sure. My parents would come and I would leave, with my son. This was my plan.

But then.

You may find this difficult to believe, so much of what went on at that time seemed odd, but it happened, or should I say it began to happen, by accident. Yes, I knew that the Vice President had resigned after his unfortunate tryst with the skater, that my husband was auditioning replacements in time for this second election on which he insisted. He seemed at that time to be winning the battle against his enemies. He would prevail again in the election and I would be condemned to this, I think you say *fish bowl*, for another term of four years. Or more, if his plan to amend the Constitution succeeded. He would talk on the plane about rebuilding the White House, had architects secretly planning, it was clear we would never escape, my son and I.

My parents came. I spent from my own account to purchase their home in Connecticut. It was my gift to them. My mother smiled and shook her head, in that way. She was proud of me, but she knew the toll. It is woman's life, she would say. But she was not a woman who could have left home on the strength of her cheekbones or a woman who had to make the difficult choices required in this country to move ahead. She thought she understood, but I am grateful that she does not.

So, to that day. I think we must begin at the night before. Or the day before, really, because that was the root of it. You may recall, there had been another shooting in another school with another of those machine guns. By one of those boys with big ears. We would have to go, fly to Kansas or Kentucky or to one of those K places and visit the hospital. When he came into my suite I was picking out pumps that I wouldn't care to wear again, the old blue Manolos, I believe. He surprised me, shoved me from behind, and I fell to my knee. He is an old man, yes, the same age as my father, but he can be quick. He called me a cow. He made a cow sound. Said he might leave me in a pasture there. I had no idea what I had done, but then I understood. The lawsuit by that woman. The judge had called him to speak. And, I later learned, on that day the attorney general had said he must testify. It was a betrayal, so everyone was against him. Me too, of course. Perhaps myself most of all. If I had been enough of a woman, he said, he would not have needed to turn to whores. He used that word. I can hear it now. I was a mother, with a newborn, such an impatient man.

I knew what to do, of course. I had learned a *technique*. I would stand and face him at attention like a soldier and look him in the eye and I would not shift my gaze. It was my only power. It did not always work, but this time it did. It was my stillness, my resolve, the truth of my real feelings. Too much for him. He said another ugly thing, but then he left and I knew he would not return.

But what I did not know, and did not learn until morning, was the awful thing. He went to my son. I had heard, of course, I knew this from his other sons, what he might do. But until this night I had been able to shield my own boy from his anger. I should have checked before bed, but at his door I heard his videogame and did not want to interrupt. We had kissed goodnight at dinner, and I knew if he needed me he would come. But not this night. On this night, he hid in his closet, like a little boy, and when I found him in the morning his lip bled from the bite of his teeth. This big man had wrestled him, I don't know why, called him a baby and a *pansy*, whatever that means. Twisted his arm until it broke. He could not understand. He was ashamed, so he did not come to me.

All that happened next came quickly. I cannot say that I remember it except as a big movie of action. I put my son to bed. I called the doctor to come now. And I rushed back into my suite in my nightgown to find something to be wearing when he came.

Yes, I will say it now, the real truth, what I have not told before.

That is when I tripped, I think on a shoe. That is when my

head hit the bedpost. That is how I was injured. I am not saying this to defend anyone. I am not saying this to change anything that has happened since. I would do it all again. So yes, I am a nasty woman. But I am not a cow.

I must have been unconscious for several minutes. My son was calling and came to me in a blur. He said, Mommy your eye. When I stood my head hurt, it was a throb like a drum at my temple and I swooned. At the mirror I saw the damage. My swollen cheek, my eye closed and quite purple and misshapen. You have seen it all. It is how I will be remembered. I have spent a lifetime before mirrors, perfecting my look, and this is my legacy. Such irony in this American life!

People do not believe me, but I will not say that I knew what would happen. I had no plan, I did not think. If you hit your head hard, if it puts you out, that is all you can think about. But I do know that I saw my son in his pajamas, holding his arm like a bird's broken wing. He does not cry now. He is almost a man. But he will allow me to say that then, just a boy, he cried. And for that, not for me, I broke.

You have seen it all. What else can I say? They did not stop me. Every man of them stood aside. I think a gun could not have stopped me that day. When I stepped onto the podium, barefoot in my nightgown, my head throbbing from the bright lights. When he turned and saw me and could not control himself. When everyone saw what we have all seen. I will always remember his face at that moment in bad dreams. The face of an *ogre*. I think that would have been enough. But then he did the other thing. He shoved me again, hard, pushed me off the stage, into the American flag and I fell with it to the floor.

I could have explained then what happened, but my son had followed me into the room, and even with his broken arm he bent to help me. It was astonishing, too, to see the Secret Service men restrain the President. They serve to protect him, but for this they pulled him back from me. When I was able to stand I said it, on camera to the world. My husband hurt my son, he broke his arm. And look at me! Look at me! This is your President!

So I didn't lie. I never said he struck me. Of course, I didn't have to. People see what they see.

No, I do not go to visit. I don't like prisons. My son went, one time, but I don't believe he will go again. We enjoy living with my parents, there is so much room, and we play music, and cook. Can I tell you what a joy it is not to care for the first time in my life what a *golaz* may do to my figure? The world will be fine. America will learn to govern itself. I think we have seen how close this nation can come to something else. I learned just now from a new book another thing that happened that day. He had wanted to push the button, but the generals stopped him. So he was angry about that, too. Enough to hurt my son. And this was my part in it. Unintentional, not *premeditated*, as some have said. But in my country we do believe strongly in what you call Fate. A thing that has to happen. Beyond our control. This was mine.

DEBBIE HAMILTON

Do you remember your first kiss? Aaron's was a late summer day before 8th grade. Debbie Hamilton. A proud name for a girl who really was just another kid, like him, ticking over into her teens. Maybe she was a little chubby, but in the lithe way of children, or maybe it was just that she had early begun to reshape, stomach squeezing up and down into surprisingly ample breasts and a rear, he later heard his father say, you could bounce a dime off. He met her in a time of great shame, and as he would learn across his life was a special womanly skill, she saved him. Short and a little pudgy himself, he'd nevertheless gone out for junior varsity football, and weeks before school started, had dropped off the team. He had been so outclassed. It had all shocked him, that there were positions, plays, techniques. Somehow he had watched NFL games on tv without ever understanding any of that. He had not even fully grasped that the game involved collisions.

The worst of it was that his pals, some of whom had been classmates since kindergarten, seemed to have figured it out. They knew how shoulder pads sat, how to tighten chin straps, had brought tooth guards to practice already softened in hot water then sucked onto their teeth for a form-fit. Where had they learned all of this? Was there some pre-JV league or something that he had missed in his goofy childhood? On top of that, football required conditioning, and again, the other boys seemed to have come prepared. Without complaint, they jogged in heavy gear and toothy cleats – he wore sneakers – around the practice field with the August sun an anvil on their padded shoulders, then dropped to a knee and leaned on their helmets at breaks exactly as NFL players did. They argued over whether it was cooler to play defense or offense and teased each other about jock itch.

Overnight, somehow, the same boys he had played kickball and dodgeball and freeze tag with on the elementary school playground had become soldiers of some kind, schooled in a complex system of stylized brutality. Because he was short, the coaches lined him up with the would-be running backs, tried to show him how to wrap the football in his arms and step with high knees, but the crush of it all was too much. In a drill, when the bigger boys came rushing to tackle him, he shut his eyes and collapsed. Everyone stopped what they were doing to laugh; the coach let the whistle drop from his mouth and shook his head. That was it. He made it through one baffling, bruising week, then went back to work at the grocery store, abashed at having failed so shamefully in his first foray at adolescence.

The grocery store sat along a rural highway amidst a peach orchard in the next county over, where Aaron knew no one, and most importantly, no one aware of his recent disgrace. His father said nothing about what had happened. It was as if he hadn't noticed. For a week Aaron had gone missing from his pickup truck on the drive across the bridge from one county to the other, and then he appeared on the passenger seat again. Aaron appreciated what he took for his father's circumspection; how could he have explained?

At the store, Aaron was the "front man". He ran the cash register, pumped gas, and made ice cream cones, all with the same unwashed hands. His father worked the back, stocking produce and butchering. They could go whole days without crossing paths except at closing time, when his father came up to the front, locked the door, and pulled the cash drawer from the register, then hauled it to the feed room where he spent an hour reconciling the books at a desk he'd rigged from a door and two saw horses.

Aaron swept the floor of all four aisles, wiped down the counters, pressed the cardboard tops back on the ice cream bins, restocked the cigarette shelves, that sort of thing, but he still had time to kill. So he had taken to riding his bike along a dirt path in the orchard at a time of day when the sky itself went peachy. By mid-August, the trees had been shorn of their fruit by the migrant workers who came into the store damp and loamy smelling for nabs, cigs, and a soda. But there were a few late peaches left in the high branches that eventually fell; each day Aaron rode along with his eye out for one perfect peach, and another for his dad that he hauled in his t-shirt around his route.

Just two days back in the saddle, still nursing the bruises from his week of shame on the football practice field, Aaron startled at the sudden appearance of a girl on a bike, peddling fast. She zoomed past him, laughing, her bare legs pumping, then stopped up ahead at a turn, one toe on the ground, to wait. Aaron almost fell off his bike, fought an urge to turn around and get back to the store. They were far out in the orchard where you couldn't even hear cars go by on the highway. The day's shadows dissolving into twilight, and the tree leaves not even trembling as if exhausted from their long day of photosynthetic oxygen production.

He couldn't just run off. He had to say hi. So he did. On the way home later, the facts began to register. Things like her dazzling sky blue eyes, her halo of frizzy hair, the dimples in her knees and at her cheeks. But in the moment it was all he could do to keep his jaw in place, as she winked and asked, "Is that a peach in your shirt?" He handed it over without a second thought, then stood straddling his bike as she accomplished a performance he'd never forget, the juice dribbling down her chin and wrist as she gnawed the fuzzy peach right down to the pit, which she then took in her mouth for a last suck, plucking it from her lips like a magic trick, then grinding it into the path with her sneakered toe. That girl really knew how to enjoy a peach.

They kicked back up on their bikes and rode. She was the one who found a replacement peach for his dad, and then she disappeared into the orchard when they got back to the highway. They hadn't swapped names, but you can be sure that Aaron was out on his bike the next afternoon, and the next, and the girl was there, too. Over the next week he learned that her name was Debbie Hamilton, and that she lived just down the road, and that she too was headed into eighth grade, and bored, and pretty much done with dolls.

It was the night of the Abingdon game. The first time in history that the Varsity team had made the state final, and the game was to be played far out in the mountains in wintry weather. The whole county went. His mother even took off work at the sewing factory to drive her table mate Sandy to the game. Aaron invited Debbie for his first real date. Darkness fell early as they drove up into the hills. The radio played Top 40 hits that tunefully, rhythmically taught the pain and joy of young love, while the women chatted up front and the wipers swiped back and forth.

On the old Impala's wide back seat, he and Debbie went to town. She seemed to already know everything. She could kiss forever, her lips soft and urgent, her tongue doing this amazing weird thing, teasing his and igniting some kind of wiring he hadn't been aware of that lit his whole frame, gluing him to her like a magnet. As the car plied the mountain switch backs, now caught up in a long line of others from the county, all headed to the football field in the mountains, one hand found itself up her blouse, then under a silky bra that lifted to this magical fullness, her right breast, a fondling gift he could hardly believe.

By all rights, they should have stopped right there. How could they attempt this private thing, he thought they called it making out, right in the back seat while his mother drove? But Debbie's kisses, the way she squirmed against him, the surprise of it all, how could they stop? Her hand went into his shirt, pulled him even closer, reached down his bare back. His other hand searched its way, he had no idea what he was doing, under her skirt, and there found itself impenetrably blocked by a rubberized wall laid down between her legs. She may have been the last girl in America to wear a girdle, but that is what she had on. So that mysterious place where a woman's insides and outsides meet, that other mouth, the vertical one, lay sealed off, unreachable. Her groin as flat and featureless as that of his sister's Barbie doll.

But a warmth seeped through. She pressed that rubberized seamlessness against his hand and took short sharp breaths at his ear, and even though he felt ridiculous, knowing that another guy, an experienced guy, would figure out what to do now, would know how to take this to the level it deserved, he just kept on with the kissing and groping, entirely out of his league, until the lights of the field filled the car, and his mother pulled in to park.

The Bobcats lost the game, a titanic defensive struggle in sleet and snow, 6-2. They'd stopped a two-point conversion attempt, had forced a safety. They'd punted on first down midway through the second half just to get their fearsome defense back on the field. His mother and her friend raved about it all as snow began to fall heavily on their drive home. Had his mother known this much about football all this time?

Debbie could have cared less about the game. After all, it wasn't her county's team. Aaron bought her a Coke and a hot dog. They huddled under a plastic tarp on the bleachers apart from his old pals, all of whom sat together in their JV jackets, howling at the most brutal tackles, joining in the cheerleader's chants, dreaming of nothing more than their eventual elevation to the Varsity team.

At half-time Debbie complained of the cold and pulled him back to the car where they immediately stretched out together on the back seat, her legs now entwining with his, and her impermeable pelvis grinding that urgent bulge at the front of his jeans. He would later learn that this relentless misery was something called *dry humping*, that its result had a name, too, *blue balls*. He woke up the next morning with swollen lips and a wrenched neck and Debbie never spoke to him again.

He walked down to her house a couple days later and knocked on her door. Her mom, standing in the doorway with an infant at her hip, said Debbie was out. He left her a sealed business-sized envelope that held a picture he'd drawn of the old oak tree in their front yard. He'd added a swing hanging from a limb and a stick figure boy pushing a stick figure girl on the swing. She flew high, her legs to the sky, while he waited with outstretched arms. It was the best tree he'd ever drawn. It wasn't just some green cloud with a brown column for a trunk; it had actual tree-like limbs that zig-zagged and attenuated into branches; he'd sketched in a shadow on the ground, and as a last thought, a basket full of peaches. He called three times, hoping she'd compliment him on the drawing, that she'd meet him for a bike ride in the orchard, or stop by the store for an ice cream. Then the other shoe dropped.

A lanky guy in tight jeans stepped out of a black *Camaro*, saying "Fill 'er up, hoss." He left the car running while Aaron pumped, the chassis seeming to pulse with the heavy bass of the music inside. The *Camaro's* windows were narrow and tinted, the cockpit so small it was more like you wore it than drove it, he thought. Aaron wondered if it had a straight shift or was just a make-believe muscle car, and when he bent to check there she sat. His Debbie, all of fourteen, strapped into the bucket seat, one hand trailing out the window cracked open on the passenger side, smoke rising from the cigarette held between her polished fingers.

Hey wait, he thought. Debbie! But before he could act, the driver came back out to the car, rolling a pack of *Camels* into his t-shirt sleeve, and held out a twenty to pay. "Keep the change, tiger," he said with a sort of half sneer that may have meant he knew. She could have leaned over. She could have rolled down the driver side window and said hi. She could have said good-bye. But she just sat hunkered in the bucket seat and smoked behind the tinted windows, as if all they'd shared, all they'd done to each other, had never happened.

When he walked back in the store after the *Camaro* punctuated his abandonment by burning a five-foot long paired stripe of acrid-smelling rubber onto the highway, his father stood waiting, as if he had known about it all along. "She's fast," he said, taking a drag on his own cigarette. Aaron knew he wasn't talking about the car. He was talking about a girl who knew what she wanted and how to get it, who understood that the game is played for high stakes with expertise, a girl who would never ride a bicycle again.

Aaron put his bicycle away, too, and when he worked at the store on weekends off from school, he walked in the orchard, kicking pebbles on the path, feeling the yellowing leaves in his bones, until at last he understood what he had to do. He talked his father into ordering a personal case of *Gatorade*. Took to running after work in the evening, on that same 3-mile loop out to the end of the orchard and back. He set up feed bags in the stock room and relentlessly practiced the one thing he'd taken from that week on the football field, crouching in a three-point stance to fire low and missile-straight, popping his shoulder hard against the bag. He'd never be a running back, he conceded that. But the Varsity coach was a stubby fireplug who had played guard in his day, and that one time he'd come by the JV practice field, he'd talked about taking down the lumbering giants on the defensive line at their knees, about pulling around end to make heroic open field blocks. That seemed doable. Next season, in 9th grade, he'd be a little bigger, he'd be in better shape. He could try again.

That's the thing about growing up. It isn't free form like childhood play. You can't just wing it and come in for dinner with a tear in your jeans. You have to learn to operate in ten-yard increments and stick to your role between the lines. You trade chub for muscle, tag for tackle, fooling around for getting 'er done. It's what the coach really meant when he bellowed, "Suck it up!" Aaron didn't know it yet, but the most important thing in his life was over; the most important thing in his life was on its way. For that, and something to do with kissing, he had Debbie Hamilton to thank.

RIVER OF DREAMS

"Hey Mark, remember that time the whole trip we did that Billy Joel song, what was it, *River of Life*, or something?"

"*River of Dreams,* man, yeah. The one with the old doo-wop bit."

"We were like Dion and the Belmonts."

"That was the shit, man."

"It was."

A lot of stuff was the shit back then. Matt almost says it, but lets the thought hang, still a little out of sorts at seeing his brother in size 50 cargo shorts and a t-shirt worn like a sausage casing, flashing on how once upon a time they had to stuff pillows up their costumes to do M&Ms for the Halloween Party at Trixie's. Wouldn't be a problem now. Matt looks out the window of the old school bus, a screen of trees in full-blown summer green smearing past. You can square up at the mirror in the morning and sort of fool yourself, but up against the real 360-degree heft of your identical twin brother, with his shirt riding up to show a belly button you could stick your thumb in, on swollen pins shoved into old sneaks, well that mirror don't lie.

But that's twins, right, it's what they all say? It's been what ten-fifteen years? Before the divorce. Before Wanda came along. The last river trip, whatever it was that happened then, it had helped make up his mind. The woods can do that, the fresh air, knocking around with the guys. It sounds pussy, but it wakes you up. And all the grab-ass, as usual that's just to prove the way it gets you in the neck before the weekend's over. Not something Mark would ever admit. He's trying to turn around and gab with the young guys in back, but can't even twist at his waist anymore, has to put one log of a leg out in the aisle, then the other, get his whole kit turned around. "Hey shut the fuck, up, Donnie!" he laughs, the old *Lebowski* line, and gets back a chorus as if rehearsed of "That's pretty Undude of you Dude!"

The cousins, the nephews, the hangers on, what ten of them, young blood, nothing like the old crew when the wives would come and it got so ridiculous, candelabras and checked tablecloths in the woods. They're doing *Forrest Gump* lines now with Jersey attempts at Southern accents, lines from *Pulp Fiction*, from *Game of Thrones*. We used to sing but that's not the way anymore. Music's over. Now it's just crap they see on tv. They can go the whole trip, no doubt, and never make up a complete sentence of their own. For every situation some dumb movie line. One guffaws a good old hillbilly laugh, hey you and Matt, y'all are just like peas and carrots! But that's not quite right. We're like peas and peas, even now with the variant burdens of 60-and change years played out on our expansive girths. Mark hears the line and huffs Matt's huff of a smile.

The bus works its way up a long grade from Matamoros, hits a winding stretch carved out of sheer cliff by the old CCC guys, their own dad among them, how the hell did they do that with just pick axes and buckets and some dynamite? It knocks you over just to think what the old guys could do. Snaky and a three-foot hand-mortared rock wall the only barrier between the narrow road and a long drop to the river. The Delaware itself breathtaking here, half a mile across, invitingly green, tree-bordered, glintingly rippled, bending off in a mist between distant hills. Even the chumps in back shut up for a minute when they see it, until one brays his appraisal, "That is one tasty burger!" It is indeed and always has been.

Mark's been planning to tell him, has been wanting to ask, but then maybe he's already guessed. One carotid blocked, some cardiac scarring, what the doctors want to do about it. After the ER scare, Brenda had urged him to call, but he hadn't and wondered now why. Maybe it would be like the time he got that crippling cramp in his leg one day, crumpled on the ground in his office clothes and only found out at Thanksgiving that Matt had sliced up his calf with a power saw at that exact moment one hundred miles away. Maybe Matt's in the same boat and he's just as freaked. Maybe they both bear the secret and equally hate it and what's there to say about it anyway? We're all time bombs whether we admit it or not.

"You're singing it, arent' ya? I can see your lips moving."

"Ha HA. When you go walkin' in your sleep. What's that next line?"

"Oh yeah it's like, In the middle of the night, when you go walkin' in your sleep...."

"De-da-de-da-de-da-de-dah. Damn, it's something. Got no signal out here or I'd check."

"That is what you'd do. And me too. Look at those knuckleheads back there. Got no minds anymore. No need to think. Remember anything."

"Google world."

"Dumb as fucking rocks."

They do their mirrored nod.

Barry, their old friend and the organizer of this trip, pulls himself free of the backseat gaggle and nudges his way forward to punch their arms. "Awesome day, huh?" he says. "Oh yeah she is. Oh yeah." For the fifteenth time he reminds them of the plan they've been talking about since February. Hit the river at noon, sandbar for lunch, pass the Pond Eddy bridge late if the water's running and start looking for their spot to set up camp. Matt tries one more time to argue for the old sandbar further downstream. That was where they used to really stretch out, make like cave men with the girls, put on the spread back in the day. But he knows Barry will have his way, and who cares really, it's all the same.

Barry was just a young pup back then, new wife and loaded for bear. He's kept his girlish figure at least a little bit, working on cars on weekends, helping the neighbors with their decks. Wife makes him eat half right. But he's got a secret too, at least from the bozos in back. She's not gonna make it, has an expiration date. Like they say about the cancer, it comes on slow until it doesn't. Who knows, she might have had it even then, little winsome thing in her bikini licking S'mores from her cheek. This trip's for Barry, the brothers had winked, a weekend to take his mind off it all for one minute. A hassle really but what the hell? You had something else to do?

Down level with the river now, rafts like enormous blue donuts spin lazy in the current, a slow motion amusement park ride packed with beer-guzzling day trippers. Guys in back leap to the window like frothing monkeys shouting "Show us your tits!" And "Dropped Your Pocket!" Already half bombed, you can hear them scrunching down their beer cans, not daring to toss them but wanting to so bad. The brothers share a knowing glance. They'll be useless in the rapids, but that first tip over will wake them up. Won't be like the old crew, but what is?

Easy to recognize the old drop off spot. Things change slower in the sticks, it seems. Candy-colored tents crammed in tight under pines, the clapboard camp store still in need of a paint job and out back the long rack of orange life vests and the stacked up blue canoes. Chill of the morning burning off and the river invitingly cool in the squish of your shoes. It takes a half hour just to haul all the gear down to the shore, an unbelievable set up, a barbecue grill and gas stove, eight-man tents meant for two, barely balled up sleeping bags, seems like one cooler per person, even some kind of portable shower thing that looks like a giant Frisbee in its wrapper. All for one night on the water. Barry patrols the half dozen canoes sprawled out in a row, giving orders like some kind of scoutmaster. Not enough bungees to go around, so pack it in tight. Keep your shit down in the gunnels. He's right to do it, and he's keeping it light, but nobody listens, they're sky high and giddy. Kids out in the water splashing, what a magnificent day.

Then this 15-year old boy with a clipboard tries to call everybody to attention, reads off the rules such as they are. Keep your life vests on. If you fall out, forget the canoe and just float. The canoe will take care of itself. Point your toes up and downstream and you'll be okay. Simple rules for a river that is a living thing, that changes day to day and bend to bend, that hides whip currents like snakes near the eddies, that ankle deep can knock you over, with under-hanging boulders and tree roots and rusty fish hooks, that on this stretch has nothing more interesting than Class One rapids – ie, nothing dangerous – and a lot of wide slow passages for lazy paddling.

To the boy Matt and Mark look like garden gnomes planted side by side in the pebbly beach, their rounded shoulders arched back against the pull of their bellies. Nobody else pays him any mind, jamming their coolers up close to the seats where they're easy to reach. The boy blows a pink bubble and straggles back up to the camp store. It's taken all morning to get to this place, but they're free now. It ain't the old days but then it is. The brothers snort their snort, catching each other in the same revery, and slap hands. Hey Frick and Frack, one of the cousins shouts, which a you lard asses is riding with me?

For the next hour it's all snapshots and grab ass, feeling it out. The old-timers slump in the backs of their canoes, shepherding the newbies up front through the ripples. The monkeys launch one first desultory water cannon assault, feeling out the guns, picking sides. One cousin unreels a pole, not expecting much. Out of a low-hanging hickory falls a bald-headed eagle, scraggly-looking thing, a juvenile maybe, almost tumbling over them as its outrageous wings unfurl to catch the air. No bird has stud wings like that.

"Dang, that's a beauty!" Mark shouts over the water. Matt and Barry nod back. Scary is what it is, like some kind of dragon with feathers. Barry yells, "Ain't it great! To see one of these guys! I mean wow!" What he means, of course, is that maybe not everything in the whole wide world goes to shit. That it just may be possible to slow the general decline, I mean if you can restore the National Bird to the skies. On the old trips you'd never see one. It was the pesticide, wasn't it, that cracked their eggs? Maybe there's a clinical trial, some kid with a test tube, I mean look at that thing take off.

When they pull up on a sandbar for lunch Mark almost says it. He and Matt end up propped against a downed tree, sharing an Italian sub and sipping their first beers of the trip, while Barry helps the dimwit with the fishing pole untangle his line and the cousins skip rocks and hoot their idiocies downstream. Matt even gives him an opening of sorts. Says, "That leg still bother you much?" Mark chews on that and his sub for a moment. "Dude, you're the one had the chain saw jump. Let me see that thing." Matt lifts up his foot and it's still a vicious gash, impressed like a toothy purple canyon in the pale melon of his calf. Matt says, "You're supposed to massage it and shit, break up the lesions or whatever, I don't know." Mark leans down to his own calf, runs a thumb down the side where the phantom scar resides. "Doctors, man, that's all they got for you. Take an aspirin, rub it down." Matt adds, "Don't call me in the morning." "No never," Mark sighs.

Matt has a secret, too, but figures he'll wait until evening after a couple shots of the single malt he's got buried in his pack, maybe go out to the old lookout rock where you sit with the people you love the most but never say that to and share the moonlit ripples and the breeze coming off the water and sort of say it that way. About this thing where back in May he'd gotten up off the riding mower, took a strangely woozy couple of steps then found himself spun around in a circle like a puppet with a broken string. Went down, got up, the whole left side of him twanging like a banged elbow, and hobbled back in the house, tried to call Wanda but couldn't read the numbers on the phone, fell out on the couch and when he woke up he was fine, it might never have happened, except the mower had sat there idling until it ran itself dry right where he'd left it out back.

He knew what that was, old man Langone down the street being the prime example, gimping along on his labored evening constitutional, stiff leg swinging that pointed toe, the cane taking some of the weight, the drooping sneer of his mouth making sounds that might be words offered in passing. Matt tells Wanda everything and will when the time is right but not yet after all she didn't marry an invalid and he's just not ready to open that can of worms. He'll go in for a checkup at some point and the shit will hit the fan and the guy he thought he was will be no more. But Mark, it's gotta be in him, too. They're on the same clock after all.

He dares another look at the full monty of his brother, and a shiver runs up the back of his damp t-shirt, a wash of the really old times that makes his eyes go wet and blink. Running crossing patterns in the yard, swiping whole frozen pies from the supermarket and breaking them in half to share, that rusty barrel they'd use to jump their bikes. All the tricks you could pull on the normals. Taking each other's tests and each other's whippings, even that one time dating the same poor girl. You can't look back and you can't help it either. It's that time of life. There just isn't any map. He wipes his eyes on his shirt and points to Barry in the water. "I'm glad we did this. Think it's good for him." Mark nods, clears his throat like he's ready to say something, then shakes his head and pops a stick of gum in his mouth.

So when it all went down, they'd never talked. Matt got it all from the coroner. Though he said he'd guessed it all along, should probably get some tests run himself. But that was days later after the shock wore off a little and the zoom of events slowed again. What happened was, they all headed back down the river, and yes what a glorious summer day it was. Drunken rafters drifted past, the water guns spouted, a pair of eagles came in low together and shot overhead like fighter jets. The clear and delicious stream narrowed at the bends and spread lake-like on the flats between sloping hills and ragged cliffs under a sky so blue it seemed to bloom.

So when Mark's canoe tipped in the first interesting run of rapids all afternoon, it seemed like no big thing. Most of the canoes made it through and were gone before they even knew it, but as Barry hit the rapids he saw Mark and the kid – what was his name? – go in, grasping for their gear amidst the crashing rocks, hanging with the hulk of the capsized boat, neither wearing a life vest. All the things they'd been told not to do. Barry tore off his vest and tossed it their way. He lost his paddle with the toss, then his balance, then his boat flipped in the torrent.

Matt and the kid with him heard the shouts and pulled off to the riverbank, then they splashed out towards the commotion heading downstream. It took four of them to drag Mark up to a rock, where one of the cousins surprised everybody with his prowess at life saving, immediately going to work pumping at the unconscious man's swollen chest. Matt stood over his brother gasping, blood hammering at his temples like fists at a door. Splayed on the flat rock, Mark lay motionless, his eyes closed peacefully as if all the troubled labor being applied to his chest was happening to somebody else. Though Matt leaned in to shadow his brother's purpling face with his t-shirt, he knew already what nobody else would admit.

Mark could have told them all not to bother. Hell, he could have told them all a lot of things. Like how a river pretty much sums up what you need to know when you think about it. Always the same, ever changing. How the little creek it was at the dawn of time still runs in the center of its wallow, how the gift it unfurls to the ocean rolls back in a circle from the sky. He could have told them that he was dissolving on the water like sugar in a coffee cup so that his very thoughts seemed to disperse to his fingertips and spurt out hosannas that popped like little fireworks in the ripples. He could have asked them to stop the CPR, the heroic pumping, but then they knew that, they were just following the rules, being heroes, all that human stuff. Mostly he wanted to share this one last thing that felt like nothing so much as love.

It took hours as it always does to get 'er done. No cell signal. Finally, the airboat from the ranger station, the unloading of canoes, the sheriff and the waivers and the coroner. Then the obscene zipping that somehow everybody saw and seemed like the final punctuation of Mark's engorged body into a sturdy orange bag. People said things. Matt told Barry, "You know I'd never say this but in a way you're blessed. Jeri knows her time, she can say her goodbyes." Barry nodded, didn't take offense. "It just goes to show," he said. "None of us really knows. There's a bullet with our name on it somewhere." A cousin who'd dived in to help drank a last beer and said, "I didn't think I was gonna make it either. The current was so strong, you'd never believe it, it was such a pretty day."

The thing about identical twins, it's that womb-deep bond nobody else understands. Matt wanted to let it all out. He knew he should cry or something, bang his head against a wall. Wanda did what she always knew to do, ran him a bath in the big tub, made him a Moscow Mule in his favorite copper cup, brought him his fluffy bath robe, and otherwise kept her thoughts to herself for now. There was never a woman like her and never would be again. In bed she held his hand and hoped to hear him snore, but as he stretched flat on his back beneath the overhead fan the crazy day spun madly behind his eyes.

And then as he described it to her the next morning, Mark came into the room with that Buddha belly like his own and with the most gentle kind of Buddha smile on his face said, "Brother let me do this one last thing, don't think it's weird, just lay there, there's something I need to check." Then Mark lay down on top of Matt. His body seeped weightlessly into his brother's, filled it perfectly to the fingertips and every hair on his arms. For the longest time they became what they'd always almost been. They were the same guy.

"I don't know," Matt said. "Maybe he wanted to see one more time what it's like on this side? To figure something he wasn't sure of? But he left me something too. He told me right to my brain, said not to be afraid of rivers. He told me to go back. And pay attention this time. And then he slipped out of me like I was just some old clothes and poofed off, left me laying there. And I gotta tell you, you'd think I'd freak or something, I mean what the fuck? But no, that's the thing. Why he came back. There's something I've been needing to tell you. You ought to know and I shouldn't have kept it to myself this long."

Matt reached for his wife's soft hand and pulled it flat to his heart, and Wanda saw the wistful smile that Mark would never make again spread on her husband's face. "You know what he said? He said, 'Matt it's okay. The water's fine.' I heard that like he was here! So look, whatever goes down, I mean whatever, don't let me forget that, okay? I love you honey. I'm good to go."

FORGETTING

"They tell me I shot myself in the chin, shot somebody else, too, but I don't think that's right. What happened was I fell off a fruit wagon."

That's Dr. Wagner. He's a pharmacist, had his own small town pharmacy out in the Valley for years, seemed fine, until this happened. I'm his occupational therapist. It's my job to determine how well he can perform his activities of daily living, things like brushing his teeth, making out a checkbook, but right now I'm conducting a cognitive screening called the O-Log. Checking for orientation to place, time, person, and situation. He's not doing too well. Problem is he's lobotomized himself with an old German Luger and can't recall that two weeks ago he shot his wife and their twelve-year old daughter, then turned the gun on himself. So he does what they call *confabulation*, makes up something that seems to make sense in the moment, and even believes it. Would be funny except.

Race home and get dressed for my brother's 30th birthday celebration at our sister's house. Leave in a huff halfway through after getting into an argument over the Confederate statues, which he has decided he worships now. Where did that come from? Out in the parking lot, my sister wags her finger along the lines of, "You don't remember much of when we were kids do you? You messed with him relentlessly and now you think he's going to listen to your shit?"

"What are you talking about?" I ask.

She drops her cigarette butt and snuffs it with one twist of a toe. "You know," she replies, pulling that drum roll of the eyes sisters are so good at.

Next morning at the hospital I monitor the old pharmacist dressing and grooming. He does fine, functioning on remote control, stuff he's done without thinking his whole life. There'll be an ugly court fight about this. The cops stationed outside his door may lead him to jail or to a mental hospital or maybe even just to a nursing home and none of it will matter a whit to him. He's got a confabulous new story for every situation and it's all just a walk in the park no matter what, which I guess is the beauty of blowing out your frontal lobes. If you don't remember it, did it ever even happen? And if it never happened, what can you make up that might have, that at least for the moment anyway explains it all?

THE JAZZMAN'S LAMENT

The drummer is a jazzman who has seen it all. He's got this old-time jive way of talking that begs an audience. Like when he says he's sucked ribs with Louis Armstrong then pauses to lick his lips in revery and recalls how sweet women would squeal just to touch a lacquered finger to Armstrong's leathery embouchure. Claims to have once stolen a jar of coconut oil from Chano Pozo, the Cuban conga drummer who was pure sex pounding out jungle rhythms shirtless in Gillespie's band, that oil making his ebony torso glisten and shimmer under the stage lights. Says he too had game in the day, once stopped the show at Condon's in counterpoint to Monk, who actually deigned to nod what he took to be approval. But in this lesser age he picks up gigs at weddings and bar mitzvah's, sometimes in Broadway or off-Broadway pit crews, keeps his hand in, his chops up, his groove on. His old hands ache from the work, but after 50 years in the business, he's just glad the phone still rings.

Because by all rights, like many of the old jazzmen, he can't see how he's still breathing. I mean, heroin, speed balls, loved the stuff. Then those scuffles with Uptown New York's Finest adding up to broken ribs, a cracked jaw, a glass eye and a limp.

Miraculously, no shattered hands, as if the brutes understood that would have been a bridge too far. The jazzman appreciates the power of his drums. He would have it known that spirits hover and are drawn like children to rhythm. Especially rhythm and sweat, rhythm made prayer by hands available to possession, by a man willed and willing to roll with it.

If you listen, if you can travel with him that far, then he stops and seems to sniff the air, gauging how much these next words will travel in the busy clinic. Then he leans in, as if crouched above his traps, and dares to speak of those things that lead in this place straight to the shrink: Devils. You see, demons with hot breath and dagger teeth have swarmed into his house, have risen to his 20th floor apartment in the artist's complex on the West Side, the one that overlooks the river, you know it. To take his young daughter. Called by the drums. So yes, he has wrestled more than one naked onyx-black tar creature with rubber muscles and flashing red eyes, has shoved them out the window, off the balcony, down roughly and gone into the icy river below, in order to save his daughter's innocent soul, because she too weak to bar the door left open by the sins of her father in a land so far away that people there have different shapes and speak in tongues.

Korea. He was a kid then, like everybody else. Like everybody else, could not get warm. But the demons remind him that he cut his captives with the tops of tin cans, dropped candle wax into their wounds just to hear them whimper. As if their foreign noise somehow explained how they all ended up in such a hell. He did that. And other things. Or says he did. Which is why, when the Boys in Blue caved in his ribs, kicked him so blood spouted out of his mouth and nose, smashed his jaw up into his eye, pummeled him in the back room of the station house as if they wished to flatten him like a cartoon character into the messy tiled floor on a Saturday night not two blocks from the club where his wife sat waiting, as they stomped and jabbed and clubbed him beyond their own dumb rage to the point of simple butt-ugly fatigue, as he went down and knew it all as some pain-dream happening both to him and out beyond him somewhere, right on the verge of death, even then as he coughed his own blood (and they lifted him like a sack and still they measured their punches and swung), he swore in his spirit-heart to the ghosts of his ancestors that he would remember this night and haunt the last days of each one of these thugs in sweaty disgusting policeman blue.

"This is how," he whispers now (that glass eye always watching the corner), "this is why I survived. Because the old ones, the ancestors, told me, 'No. You cannot come. You must settle this on your side of the grave.' They told me, 'Live and heal.'" Then they gathered in a council about him, above the fray, and threw him back to the wolves. But this he kept from them, held deep in his wounded heart, a heart made black by all he had done, a heart that could not atone, except in this way. He would awaken broken and one-eyed and limp all the rest of his days, but hoped as the beating wore down that they would do their worst.

"You see," he says, "I swore to them, 'I curse you. You will never rest another night undisturbed or know another season of good health. All your loved ones will fade to smoke in horrible ways that will break your soul until you die alone to be buried in a grave without flowers on a bleak plot entirely unmarked and forgotten. You will walk the spirit world as one shunned across eternity, scorned even by the shades that are most despised on the other side. At the same time I plead for each of your beastly, race-hating, meat packer strong, bullying blows. I tell you my fathers, this is what I have lived for, walked the edge of, craved without ever knowing that I did. And here it is, the answer, my teeth like loose corn in my mouth.'"

He says they did him a favor and to this day believes they knew it. Says that something wild and beastly came unleashed in them that night, that even though they had beaten down Hispanics and blacks and Eyetalians every weekend shift of their brief careers and would again until their shoulders gave way from years of pounding, that this was the pinnacle they would seek across all the whippings to come, that one night when it really got good to them. "See," he explains, "that was the night they walked with me into a place I inhabited alone, that I knew as I know my drums. I held the door for them, helped them down in the hole, and brutes that they were, how could they resist? Which, of course, is when I had them. And now they too will never rest."

I don't really know what to say to all that, so I just do my job. I unwrap the towels and peel the gummy paraffin from his aging, powerful hands. His perfectly manicured fingernails gleam as he wriggles his fingers in pleasure. "Ah, good as getting a nut," he sighs. I drop the balls of wax back in their vats, toss the towels in the bin and turn back to him. I have to ask, "Did it help? This penance of yours, when the cops almost killed you. Have things been different since then?"

The jazzman stretches out his thick fingers and flattens his hands on the table, as if to examine their sheen. "Ah, young man, you have never been to war. How can I tell you this? You see, what I learned that night, you will not understand, but think on this if you will. I was mistaken. The living thing they beat, it was not me. My penance, as you call it, lies elsewhere. It waits for me in an icy trench with candles that throw shadows on the wall. All these years, I've been waiting in line. And when my time comes, then I will go."

THE BIRD MAN OF CENTRAL PARK

There was a bird at the window, tapping. The heat pipe radiator squeezed between the bed and the wall hissed itself awake, as it always did at dawn, steaming the window, which then frosted in overlapping snowflake patterns that would finally melt only when that one glimpse of pale sunlight peaked over the brownstone opposite around noon. The bird was tapping its hard black beak on the frosted window, as if it thought the glass was a sheet of ice covering a puddle somehow stood up vertical. No more unusual, certainly, than other adjustments one must make to survive in the city, an aviary that features electrified perches, daylight at night, noxious fog, hurtling metal boxes on wheels....

Terrence DeKalb lay inside the window on a creaky single frame bed, his enormous bulk napkined by a wool blanket that left his feet sticking out, a situation only partially eased by heavy wool hiking socks. He waved a beefy hand at the window and whispered, "shoo," as if to a lover. But the bird paid him no mind. So he reclined there inches from its insistent pecking, observing the performance cock-eyed. This was a method he'd learned from birds without realizing he had done so. The frosted pane blurred the bird's shape, made it just an insistent shadow. He guessed a sparrow, maybe of the white-throated variety. The bird paused, as if listening. DeKalb waited, too. He could never tell if in moments like this there was some kind of communion, sharing for an instant the nature of a feathered thing, the exhilarating emptiness of avian consciousness that must be like some exquisite awakened exaltation. Thought like flight and vice versa.

It was a moment of not even breathing. He imagined himself the mountain over which the blackbird flew in that poem taped to his refrigerator, 20 *Ways of Looking at a Blackbird*. But he could not hold his breath or hold the thought forever. It was so hard to focus. And with that the bird threw open its fisted self and was gone, leaving only the milky window, the gray walls, the hissing radiator, the overburdened cot, and a man exhausted – even after ten hours abed – beyond fatigue.

DeKalb was tired for a biological reason that sleep could not cure. His muscles, even during the night, chewed away at themselves. The chemicals that made up his body had gone rogue, lactic acid eroding the motor cells even of his toes and eyelids. Any effort at coordinated movement involved a mighty heave of courage. To climb out of bed required calibrations of glacial magnitude. Every morning, he fought this lonely war. But the bird, he imagined, had come as a courier meant to call him forth to the day, and for this herald he would gather his dwindling resources and again attempt to do what was needed.

He followed a routine laid out serendipitously over the years but rigidly adhered to now, each step measured for economy of motion, for energy conservation. Donning his clothes incorporated an evaluation of gas in the tank, a calculation of what might be available today in the way of gross motor skill. If it had only been about him, he would never have bothered. It would have been so easy to just lie there listening to the radiator until the hissing faded away. But wild things with the brilliant energies of flight and song depended upon his appearance on each wintry morning. So for that he gathered whatever momentum he could marshal and sallied forth to the park.

The tedious process of dressing, then daring the negotiation of two rickety flights of narrow stairs, the heavy metal door to the street, and the icy stoop left him dizzy and gasping. But he forced himself to go on until at last his feet found their rhythm, shuffling along with an unthinking regularity. Bundled in his stained and pockmarked down jacket, in his khaki slacks over long johns, the old fedora with ear flaps, water-proofed boots and wool gloves with their fingers cut out for dexterity's sake, DeKalb made his way to the park entrance where he paused to suck at the searingly cold air and delight at the twin vapor trails streaming from his nose. His old lungs still pumping, pushing oxygen out to the remnant cells that still cared, those that had not yet rebelled against their host.

In his backpack, he hauled a pound of lard, Manteca, suet, whatever you want to call it, wrapped in butcher paper. The front pocket held his medicine bottles filled now with sunflower seeds, kernels of corn, peanut butter and nuts. And in the crook of one arm, he carried a new feeder for a dark corner of the Ramble, meant to replace one torn down by greedy squirrels. DeKalb had spent months perfecting a pest-proof feeder and felt that his latest invention was the simplest, most economical and elegant contraption he had yet devised. But squirrels acting in gangs might still launch themselves from ice-stiffened branches and drag the thing to the ground with relentless, determined leaps, unless he found the perfect place to hang it.

Placement was everything, yet there simply wasn't enough clear space amidst the boulders, pin oaks, and barberry bushes to deny his enemies a launching ramp. Yes, the squirrels were his enemies, but only because at an early stage DeKalb had chosen sides, recognizing the necessity of narrowing one's ambitions within the realm of the possible. He had met a young man who patrolled the city with a net, capturing feral cats and seeking homes for them in the suburbs. School children and old maids brought peanuts to benches all over the park to feed the ravening squirrels. But managing the needs of the city's aerial occupants was not so straightforward a proposition. Each breed of bird had its own proclivities and tastes, its own favorite food. He understood the over-wintering types – the chickadees, the sparrows, the cardinals and jays – and made sure to bring the easy to crack sunflower seeds and grain for them. But his choice entailed attention to the specialized diets of migrating flocks, too – protein-rich grubs for the mergansers and snow geese, sugar water for hummingbirds – though in the dark months of deep winter those flocks were long gone, and it was just the birds he called the residents he served.

It was not enough to bring food, of course. He had learned where to place it, how to shelter perches from careening hawks, how to make this unnatural provision seem to have grown from the earth. So he smeared the crunchy peanut butter the downy woodpeckers love as high as he could reach in the seams of a hickory, he scattered seeds on the wind, he had even concocted this sling-shot apparatus he would take on its trial run today, hoping to wing a knob of suet far out over the high limb of a tulip tree where it would catch and hang like a spent yo yo only creatures with feathers could reach. It would take a mighty heave; he knew it would tax his last reserve. But then if he could just get to the subway and make it down to 23rd Street for his weekly infusion, then he'd recover. He would lounge idly in the warmth of the infusion room, amidst the other systemically-wounded veterans snuffling and snoring in reclining chairs, as the fiery chemicals pulsed into his veins. For another couple of days he wouldn't have to face that impending horror, a mummy slowly stiffening on an icy park bench. And while he was away for his hospital sleep over, his feathery charges would have the sustenance they needed to tide them over from any brewing blizzard.

The epidemiologist called it genetic, this slow muscle-wasting death march of his. Mitochondrial disease. But that was the usual BS, delivered with an administrative wink, since the VA had chosen to treat this incurable and purportedly hereditary illness as 100% service connected. Because a hundred flights dumping plumes of Agent Orange on a tropical jungle, wearing just a bandanna to cover your face when you leaned out the chopper door to tip an emptying barrel…. Even the VA didn't fuck with that any more. They tagged it a *presumptive* service connection, edging towards a sidewise admission. But that was just the usual bureaucracy. Nothing they were ever going to do would extinguish the sapping fire in his organs, the wailing fatigue in his muscles, the spinning colors or the splitting headaches. And nothing he was ever going to do would pay for the voluptuous rainforest he'd burned to wilted desert with those billowing orange clouds that had stifled the breath from every living thing they touched. Now even with eyes closed he saw them, all the time, flocks of birds tumbling out of the air.

Maybe you ran across him that day down the hill from Belvedere Castle? Say you had finished your jog around the reservoir and chose to add a little fartlek variety to the morning, whipping up and down the narrow lanes of the Ramble? But then you slipped on a shard of ice and thought better of your plan, slowing to a walk with your gloved hands further sheathed in the pockets of your running jacket, as you pretended for one moment that this rectangle of woods compressed between walls of brick was a wild place, laughed at your silly pretension and turned to sorting your plans for the busy day ahead. And there he stood.

Later you recounted how this bear of a man, wrapped in

ballooning down clothing so he looked like some giant Eskimo statue or something paused beneath a mighty tulip tree and began with what seemed like great ceremony and titanic effort to turn on his axis, grimly accelerating as a rope with what looked like a bowling ball or something at its end swung out in the air and then with a sudden upturning release the slingshot or whatever it was soared straight up on the energy of the spin, trailing some kind of peg or hook, shot over a high branch above the path, caught in a fork and then hung swinging like a gob of phlegm far up and suspended way out in the air.

And then the man sat flat down in the crusty snow hunched like a melting snowman but breathing hard and vapor rising like smoke from his head so you wondered if you should ask and did that familiar hesitant half step forward with a hand out but then stopped dead in gathering wonder as first one then another bird flitted down and landed right on him. A ragged pigeon, then another, on one arm. A mourning dove, a flock of little brown jobbies, on his knees and shoulders. A seagull that seemed as big as an eagle alighted right on top of his hat and let loose with its caustic laugh. I mean in like one minute this guy was positively festooned with birds! They reached in his pockets and seeds sprayed all around. More birds flitted in from everywhere it seemed. And you're gonna think I'm nuts, but when he came to a stand again, it was almost as if they lifted him up. They were all flapping their wings and grabbing him with their little claws and their beaks.

Back on his feet he stretched out his arms like a hulking fat scare crow, except it was just to give them a better perch. They ate from his outstretched hands. The seagull hopped off his head and stood squawking for a moment at his feet. It flew around him in a circle, then sailed away. I followed his eyes up to that thing he'd thrown up in the tree, and already a couple woodpeckers were perched there, hammering away at whatever was in it. I wanted to say something, to speak to him, but he seemed all wrapped up in his work, and I didn't want to chase the birds away. He was still standing there, and birds were still coming, when I left. I know you won't believe me, it was just amazing.

No, stop, I totally get it. I've seen him, too. A lot of people have. Congratulations, grasshopper, and welcome to the city. After all, it's not the Empire State, the Statue of Liberty that matter to those of us who call this burg our home. It's these encounters, always. Consider yourself baptized. You have now witnessed one of our great unsung wonders – the Bird Man of Central Park.

LET IT SNOW

"Don't fight me, Sweetie. Let me help."

Ben protested, or tried to, but his words were muffled by the turtleneck shirt Sarah sleeved down his head, pausing to smooth his sleep-tousled hair with one motherly stroke before taking his ruined arm at the wrist to fit his fist up the rumpled folds at his shoulder. He sighed, she hadn't understood, which was just as well. He'd only been bitching, one of the few things he could still manage on his own. She loomed above him now, smelling of a loamy bed warmth, her breath a little rank, having yet to brush her teeth. Leaning in, she clasped his thick fingers in hers and helped him shove his weak arm to the end of the sleeve, releasing his hand as it popped through at the end then retracting her own back through to the shoulder.

"I can do this side, just stop will you?"

She stepped back. Not yet dressed and already testy, but then of late. She waited behind the chair, poised to help if needed. It was this austere tableau, a pale end of year light through the lace curtains that turned the bedroom's blue walls a drowsy lavender, and that wintry early morning hush when even the birds were still sleeping. In their silent water-colored box, a bed and a wheelchair and a long married couple doing this necessary thing. They might have lain abed and let the day go, but here they were, back at it again. He bit his lip and with a long-tested pride tunneled his good arm through the sleeve without incident. She stepped forward then, swift as a dancer, and as he leaned away in the chair tugged the shirt down around his torso to his waist.

She finished at the front of the chair, perching briefly at bed's edge, and puffed at a wisp of hair going silver across a forehead creased with fine horizontal lines. Though neither knew it at the time, the searching gaze that linked their eyes for a brief moment in that ghostly light before she bent to kiss his nose good morning was the last time they would share a soulful glance. "I'll get the suppository," she said.

Sarah would be running all morning, putting the house in order for the after Christmas party they'd thrown for years, beginning when the kids were toddlers and the neighbors in what was then a brand new development out in the woods brought their own kids and boxes of Santa presents that all got dumped in the family room together like a toy store turned upside down while parents sated with the success of their subterfuge downed flavored bourbons they'd gifted each other and talked over the candied sounds of holiday CDs jingling for the last time that year. The kids were grown now, some had children and traditions of their own, so the party had petered out with time to a mostly old fart event, starting earlier in the day and running later. The men blasted their new shotguns out back; the women swapped gift cards and helped Sarah take down the tree, then they all shared ham and sweet potatoes and pecan pie left over from everyone's Christmas dinners, and sat fat and happy in the detritus of the way we Americans play.

This year, for the first time, Ben couldn't do much to help. He sat at the breakfast table, not really attending to the flurry of action at the feeder out on the porch, and sipped his second coffee feeling more than ever like a fifth wheel. Sarah got that and tried, she really did. "Sweetie, will you answer the phone? People will be calling all day. It's so cold, pipes are bursting, folks will ask what to bring." He could care less that the woodpecker had found the suet, that the blue jay cop who kept everything in order seemed to be off duty, leaving the plump red cardinal to lord it over the chickadees. Already bored with asking silly questions of their new *Echo*, he ordered the polite black cylinder to play a bluesy Christmas channel and nodded along, feeling like a misfit toy.

The blessing they say is that you can't remember it. He'd gone to the site, of course, and sat at the edge of the road looking down at the tree that had stopped their car. It had been month's later and whatever tracks there were had grown over in the green effulgence of a Virginia summer, but the old white oak proved it well enough, its thick trunk still naked as flesh where the impact had stripped off the bark. If you looked, you could still find singed branches down low. He'd gone out the side window, his spine snapped mid-back by the door, and landed out cold fifty feet from the car. Caroline, dear Caroline, and her best friend Jazmin, both in their soccer gear, trapped in the back seat in the fire. Who knows what happened? No one ever came forward. Blown tire? Deer crossing the road? An instant of inattention fiddling with the radio? It didn't matter. They were gone and he was broken. She'd had ten girlish Christmases, now twenty since without her. Thank God for Billy her little brother, but what a burden he'd had to bear.

Ben tried to recall what it had been like at first after the car wreck, in the early weeks of discovering what a severed spine can mean. That odd constriction below the nipples, as if his pants had been pulled up tight and cinched there at the sudden demarcation line for touch. Swooning whenever the physical therapist swung his legs down to the floor, that edge of madness frantic effort at good cheer, racing his hand-me-down wheelchair along the hospital corridor in a desperate ploy to pretend it was all just a video game or a vivid dream he'd awaken from with morning.

This new shock felt just as cruel, except by now he knew better than to fake it. Here was the line he'd sworn not to cross. Yes, it was true, he'd shown them all. Take away ambulation, take away standing to pee, take away anything like normal sex. The stack of Christmas cards on the hall table proved what he had achieved. A hero and role model to people with spinal cord injuries all over the state, the one who showed everyone that there can be life after wheelchair. *When you came into my room that day and handed me a tennis racket my life changed forever. I'll always be grateful for the talk you had with my wife. Remember how we all lined up and blocked the door to the men's room at the state house until those asshats agreed to hear us out? Dude, you gotta come back and join the basketball team again. You started it. It just ain't the same without you. Remember, man, like you always said, where there's a will there's a way.*

When the phone rang he ordered Alexa to shut the fuck up so he could talk. The music ended so abruptly it was as if he had slapped her phantom face. So that's what robots are for, he thought, lifting the phone to his ear. Jared, one of his great protégés. Ordinarily, it would be great to hear his cheering salesman's voice.

"Ben, look, are you sure it's okay to bring the kids? I mean, it's three now and they can be a handful."

"Are you kiddin', man? You always come. It'll be more like the old days, seriously, don't even think of it."

"Okay, then I'll tell Trish you said so. She knew that's what you'd say. Yo look, I got news. Christmas Eve, when they all got settled down at last, we decided to bite the bullet. We're gonna adopt all three, the two toddlers and Camila, you remember her, she's five now."

"Dang, dude, wow."

"I don't know. They're sweethearts, really, and Camila we've just been fostering for six months, but we really think."

"You guys are the real Santa's, you know that, right?"

"Got it all from you, buddy. Day One."

"Well we never did that, man."

"Well, you had your own kid, and you did right by him, too."

"They're not coming."

"No? Well with the snow heading this way, probably a good thing. That's a long drive from Philly."

"Yeah. We *Facetimed* with 'em last night. It's mostly the baby, she's got a flu or something, croupy. Bummer, though."

"They love you man. Grandpa rocks."

"Rock-n-roll. Yeah. Not so much with this fuckin' arm."

"Shit, what'd they say? I shoulda called you."

"Man, if you saw the x-rays, it ain't pretty. Whole shoulder's hangin' by a string. Said rotator cuff erosion, just waitin' for it, and when the chair tipped. I shoulda gotten that other one from you, man, it just wasn't cambered right."

"It was tennis? You were playing up with the T-12's, weren't you?"

"Whatever. I couldn't even get up. Felt like a cleaver went through my shoulder."

"Damn."

"They said the biceps tendon tore right off the bone, whole muscle just curled up in a ball at my elbow."

"Shit, are you kidding?"

"And this time they can't stitch it back so it'll work again. My doc, check this out, he said, "Well, Mr. Morris, one option would be amputation.""

"You're shittin' me."

"The whole arm's dead, man. It's just fucked."

"What are they gonna do?"

"That's it. They can't. Too torn up. They can pin it but it'll be useless. Got me on oxy, but I won't take it. Hurt's like a bitch. Do not say that to Sarah."

"So you're the one-handed gimp."

"That's it. That's the thing. No legs, the bum arm, one that still works, but I'm not a lefty. So Sarah's dressin' me and pushin' me around like a baby. She's gotta tip me into the car, onto the shower seat. Catheter, man."

"Dude. Stop. We can fix that. We got one-arm chairs at the store. And come on. I been after you to go motorized for years. There's no shame in it."

"Makes sense for you, you broken neck C-6 bitches."

"Dude."

"I don't know. Look, come on tonight. Sarah cooked enough for us all twice over. It's just a thing."

"It is that."

"Bring the kids, all of 'em. Adopting. Proud of you, man. That's a big step."

"It is that."

"It's what Christmas is all about, right? Y'all come on."

After the call, Ben felt raw. The thing he hated most in the world was complaining. He sat at the table where Sarah had pushed him, his face distorted like a shadowy ogre's in the laptop's blank screen. He could make himself marginally useful scanning *Facebook* and firing off a few emails out of her way while she did everything else. Even last year, he'd vacuumed and dusted, baked a row of his famous pies – the pecan and chocolate chess and lattice-crusted apple – but you can't push the wheelchair and the vacuum cleaner with just one hand, and there's no such thing as a one-armed rolling pin. Useless. Jared was right, of course. A lot of people out there worse off than he was. All sorts of ways to make it work. Hell, there's probably even voice-controlled shower lifts now, if he wanted to go full invalid. But the one device Sarah had dared to give him, wrapped like a real present under the tree, that transfer strap for the car, he'd acted like a fool, winging it across the room in anger. She'd stomped off to the bedroom and slammed the door, leaving him abashed in the twinkling lights of the tree, thanks to him the worst Christmas morning they'd had in years.

"What's wrong with me?" he one-finger pecked onto *Facebook*, then deleted it before hitting Enter. Not the sort of thing people share on that forum, even if half of us feel it half the time. Not at Christmas time. He reached over to the dead arm and tenderly fingered the knotted bulge above his elbow that felt firm as a tennis ball wedged under the skin. You could stroke it or leave it alone and it still hurt. The hand worked, but without an arm to lift it that modicum of function seemed just a nuisance. If I was young again, he thought, if I was still concussed and didn't know better, then yes, I could learn a whole lot of ways to make it work. Like I learned how to dress, to drive, to pull a wheelie. *"What's wrong with me?"* he typed again.

When everything was ready, and the whole house fragrant as a gift shop from her finishing touch, hot apple cider with cloves and a cinnamon stick bubbling on the stove, Sarah wheeled him into the bathroom for their bath. It helped his mood to have her with him in the big walk-in shower, both of them slippery and glistening, her breasts firm as rubber ducks and her hands electric at his neck and shoulders. When she stood before him to scrub his hair, water blasting her back and steam fogging their little world, he gripped the grab rail hard and leaned precariously in to kiss the old Caesarian scar branded like a sacrificial smile into her abdomen. She giggled girlishly, misjudging his tenderness as a come on, and stepped closer, right up against his grizzled face that knew everything there was to know about her.

She towered above him, a lithe, pink, fruited banquet, and it crushed him deliciously anew to have only his lips and tongue and chest to savor it all. One arm lay dead in his lap, the other gripping the grab rail for dear life. Another treasure lost in the topple on the tennis court.

Sarah intuited that shift, pulled away and bent to kiss the top of his head, then scrubbed up a mountain of suds there and blasted it off with the hose. She went about her work with a nurse's efficiency, finishing him and shampooing herself, then rinsing them both, the water streaming down her sturdy legs. It had been years since he'd allowed a tear to fall, but he could not stop them now. Fortunately, in all the busy fog, she didn't notice, and by the time she stepped out of the shower, toweled herself dry, tucked one in at her breast and made a turban of another, then came to tip him forward and reaching around, his chin at her moist and fragrant shoulder, dabbed at his rear end, then pivoted him neatly from tub bench to wheelchair, he had steeled himself to the day's travails. Crybaby. He had never allowed that luxury before, and would not weaken to it again, not with all he had to do.

The Henderson's, as always, were the first to arrive, blocking the slate walk with their salt-blasted Buick, then emptying themselves helplessly into the sheeted snow, trying to decide whether to risk the ramp or the steps. They took the ramp, Nellie's arm clasped tightly at Al's elbow, and observed from the front picture window, their travail up that long incline with its inch of new snow appeared fraught with all the struggle of an Alpine ascent. Nellie dug her chin deep in a woolen scarf, Al grasped the rail with his gloved free hand and tugged as if on a guy rope with each daring step, but eventually they made it, and stood triumphant at the threshold loathe to glance back at the treacherous terrain they'd traversed. Ben swung the door open on its automatic hinge before they could reach for the bell. They blinked in surprise at his welcoming smile. "How did you know we were here?"

"Come in. Come in," he grinned, one-arming the chair towards them, so it pivoted instead of rolling forward. "Drop your galoshes there on the mat, the door will close itself, no problem. Here, hand me your coats." But then Ben realized that, no, that won't work, and as the heavy wool overcoats landed on his lap, all he could do was sit and wait for Sarah to collect them. This will never do, he thought. I'm a human coat rack, plopped in the middle of the foyer and blocking the door. The Henderson's, for their part, didn't seem to notice, Nellie determined to unload her well-rehearsed apology for having arrived at a potluck empty-handed, Al angling already for the kitchen and some nibble as if he had not eaten all day. She began, "Oh, my dear hubbie had the last egg for breakfast yesterday and our road, you know it's bad on a good day, well the plow didn't come until near dark. I just won't let Albert go out, his eyes are not what they were, and you can't make a chess pie without eggs!"

Sarah, in her creased jeans and the plaid flannel shirt she'd unboxed in that unsuspecting yesterday of gently falling snow with the aroma of fresh coffee and cinnamon buns – when the new Echo lay dumb on the floor and that damned misunderstood car door strap sat wrapped in Ben's lap – bent now to relieve him of the overcoats, her head cocked to the old familiar exculpation. Nellie was her mother's last surviving sibling – the youngest of six – and she would never change, poor helpless thing that she was. "Come in," Sarah beckoned, then gave Ben a quick peck at his forehead, leaving the indelible print of her freshly painted lips at his hairline, a seal of affection he would wear unknowingly all night.

As the women veered off to the living room to admire the tree, Ben pivoted his chair in a semi-circle to face the kitchen where Al had disappeared, then thought, No, he'll take care of himself. This is exactly where I should be, planted at the door with my *Open Sesame* controller, greeting all comers, and out of Sarah's way. And that's where he sat for the next hour, though as new folks arrived and bent for hugs or a lefty hand shake, he found his chair gradually edged away from the door, so by the time the living room and kitchen were jammed with friends and the mingled fragrances of their new colognes, he had ended up in the passageway between them, and they had to walk around.

Most of the talk at first centered on the welcome white Christmas they'd all had, the first in a decade, it's importunate brown outs and driveway drifts providing just the right level of crisis to raise everyone's spirits. Troy, Ben's second in the *Blue Cross-Blue Shield* IT department, owned a plow extension for his F-150, and he'd spent the day going down the list of party guests, digging them out, then moving on to the next, accepting only a toddy in recompense, thus arriving well-lit at the doorway, his quite young girlfriend Amy at his side. Troy deposited her at the door, where she stood shyly in the foyer – this was her first time – while he rummaged in the garage, found a shovel and spent the next half hour scraping snow and ice from the ramp and front steps, then salting them from a 20 lb. bag he sprinkled in a practiced sweeping motion that reminded Ben, watching fondly at the window, of his grandfather feeding chickens back in the day. No one had asked Troy to do this; it was his way both at work and after hours. If Troy had a religion -- he was not a churchgoer -- it was to make himself useful, head on a swivel, always ready to fill a need. If he could only learn to delegate, give up control of some small things, he'd make a good manager one day.

Larry, their nominal boss, arrived in his imposing four-wheel drive *Escalade* just as Troy was stowing the shovel, and he waited with his wife Laquisha in the drive, accepting a drunken bear hug with an eye-rolling smile, and stomping his snowy boots at the doorway disarmed, unofficial, and for the first time all day in something of a holiday spirit. Layoffs loomed at New Year's, the names of the doomed on a list in his office at home, good men who dug under desks and came up with dust bunnies in their hair. He'd spent the day alone and fretful, pacing the den while his wife had been off with her sisters returning gifts at the Short Pump Towne Mall. But he'd promised her to set his worries aside for the party, to somehow make these hours a bubble apart. Troy's over-friendly hug made that easier. He squeezed Laquisha's mittened hand at the door and gave her a conspiratorial wink. She leaned into his arm and prepared herself with an exaggerated sigh for the foolery of white people just inside the door.

Which came promptly. Ben's oldest friend Buster, a lineman on the high school football team he'd half-backed for, had parked out back to make a surprise grand entrance. He sneaked in the kitchen door to launch himself at the Christmas tree adorned head to toe in the not inconsiderable gift his doting wife Linda had dazzled him with one day ago – the full parade attire of a Confederate Army Colonel, replete with feathered cap, dangling shoulder sash, brass buttons, buttery leather gauntlets, and the cavalry sword he now brandished wildly, like some tv musketeer, while unreeling the ungodly shriek all the best reenactors agreed best approximated the storied *Rebel Yell* battle cry from the Civil War.

Just as he must have hoped, Buster's outrageous masquerade broke the party open like the smashing of a pinata, providing the childish shove all needed to throw off their new-sweatered *Oh Holy Night* decorum and fall happily down into the sugary cheer the holiday yearns toward. All raised their glasses in relief as the oaf in dress grays took a deep bow, and by the time he'd gathered himself to scabbard his sword, tuck his hat at an elbow and ceremoniously unglove, people were kicking off their shoes, pecking at cheeks, wiggling a little at the holiday playlist, and finding themselves giddily glad to have come all this way again. Laquisha, for her part, shook her head in mock dismay and took a good pinch of the flesh at Larry's middle. The girls at Zuumba, she knew, would roll at this tale!

The last to arrive, Ben had almost thought they'd miss the party entirely, were the Collinses, the only guests with children in tow. They appeared at the door grouped like a *Unicef* Christmas card photo, Trish with one hand on Jared's shoulder and the three children, all of different ethnicities -- Asian, African American, and Hispanic -- surrounding his wheelchair, shy and giggling, while glittering snowflakes drifted about them. Ben sat momentarily stunned at this domestic tableau, so charming, so hard earned, so rich with event, and found tears again coming to his eyes. Jared saw that, instantly understood, looked around at his family on the stoop and shouted, "We bring tidings of good cheer!" He nudged his joy stick, launching himself into the foyer, and the others flowed in around him.

With the Collinses' arrival, Sarah winked at Ben and returned to the kitchen to bring out the hot buffet. There was food everywhere it seemed. Across the kitchen counter stretched the favorite salads of America's decades, each a specialty of the guest who had brought it – the Pulliam's Caesar (with hand-chopped and toasted croutons), two versions of molded *Jello* (the Miller's layered in stripes of red and green, the Stovall's imbedded with fruit cocktail and topped by a glistening sour cream icing), Meg Ross' snowy Waldorf chunked with grapes and Mexican watermelon, and its Ambrosia sister a la Kathy Kent plump with baby marshmallows. On a side table sat the overflow, an untagged bright yellow potato salad poxed with paprika, a Greek-style 3-bean with black olives and feta, and a Caprese with roasted red peppers instead of out of season tomatoes.

One side of the dining room table held casseroles: macaroni and cheese, tomato sauced ziti, corn pudding, turkey dressing, and cheesy stuffed peppers, while the other side bore an assortment of partially-eaten pies – pecan, lemon meringue, chocolate chess, apple, and mincemeat – and cakes – German chocolate, cheesecake, pineapple upside down, and hummingbird -- along with several plates piled with mixed Christmas cookies and fudge. These the only remnants of the party's original intent, to share leftovers with friends in the afterglow of Christmas. Everything else, of course, had been prepared especially for this event.

Rylie Ellis, the young realtor and school board member – who had been a close friend of Ben and Sarah's daughter Caroline all those years ago – must have risen early to thinly slice and scallop potatoes for a perfectly browned and creamy French casserole. She fretted, as always, that they were overcooked, but Laquisha laughed, "I like my gratin dauphinoise the way I like my men, dark and tasty!" So all was well.

A fold-out sideboard held crescent rolls, beaten biscuits, zucchini and banana breads, and a few store-bought lengths of baguette. Then, of course, the liquor shelf dazzled, the men vying to upstage each other. There would be no target practice in the backyard this evening, with the temperature dropping by the hour and new snow sifting out of the darkness. Anticipating that, all had brought instead of a rifle a fresh bottle of a favorite whiskey to share, along with six packs and wine, hard cider, and lemonade for the youngsters. Eyeing the dinner spread with foot-tapping patience, they tossed pretzels and nuts into their mouths with bourbon chasers, shaking their heads in amusement at the three surprisingly well-behaved kids, who sat happily plopped in a corner by the Christmas tree, thumbing their new screens.

At last, Sarah enlisted Buster to haul out the *Smithfield* ham she'd been doctoring most of the week. The first day, she'd scrubbed the ham's moldy hide, then she'd soaked the disgusting pink haunch for two days in cider and *Coca-Cola* before boiling the meaty thing in two changes of water to desalt it, finally glazing the surface with brown sugar and cloves for its finishing roast in the oven. All evening the ham's mouth-watering fragrance had dominated the cedar and cider and other holiday smells throughout the house. Buster hefted the ham with regal deference across the kitchen floor, careful to keep the platter away from his officer's jacket that was yet unblemished by the rigors of role play on some battlefield of yore. He set the evening's entrée at Ben's cutaway table, awaiting his old friend's ceremonial carving and prayer of good cheer.

It was then that Sarah gasped at yet another mistake. How could she have failed to foresee this? No way Ben could carve the ham in his current state! But here he came rolling, bedecked with a necklace of Christmas lights, a gift from that darling Camila, the oldest of Jared's children, and pushed by Troy, who pretended to be skating his stockinged feet across the tile floor while happily singing, "Over the River and Through the Woods". Then everyone, it seemed, joined in the old song, swaying together around the ham. Thankfully it was a short tune, or at least as much of it as people remembered. Troy handed the thick electric knife into Ben's good left hand, steadied the ham himself with a kitchen fork, and Ben bent to the task as always, letting the whirring tool do the work of neatly slicing juicy slabs that flapped down across the knife blade. Troy then nudged him to turn off the scissoring action while he lifted each slab to a serving plate. Hand to her mouth, Sarah hovered behind them, watching the two friends find a new way to complete this old routine. This is how it could be, she hoped, if only.

And then it was time for the benediction. Ben lay the greasy knife on a platter now splattered with scraps along the unfortunate hog's thick femur. Larry, his boss, popped open and handed him a canned beer for the toast. Ben paused to look around the kitchen at all the old friends gathered once again even on this snowy December evening when they might just as well be watching *Netflix* in their jammies, and simply thanked them for coming. Some years he prepared a homily or a self-penned poem or rap, but this time he seemed choked up, bleary eyed, at a loss for any words that might sum up what all these people had come to mean in the mediated disaster of his life. He had hoped, without admitting it to himself, that their coming this year would prove something, would mark a turning, but if so he hadn't felt it yet. He raised the can to shoulder height, intoned the five words that his daughter had scrawled on a card long ago and that had eventually become his mantra, "It's all about the love." Then strangely exhausted, he lowered the can to his lap and simply nodded for the gluttony to begin.

"It's all about the arrangement," old man Al chuckled as he constructed a sloppy pyramid on his plate. "You need a solid foundation, that's a good slab of ham, and then some corn pudding next to this macaroni, so it'll grip. Then you can go ahead with some fried apples on top of that, maybe a little ambrosia, top it off with a buttered roll."

"Well, yes, but for me," replied Linda, "I like to balance the flavors and the textures just so. I put all the salty over here, and the sweet on the other side, and anything crunchy down the middle. See here's my ham slice, and my Caesar salad (it's so good with these toasted walnuts!), and this sliced potato salad thing run right down the middle. I don't like to have them touch until they get in my mouth!"

"Y'all don't know what's good," Buster laughed, looming beside them with a plate full of dessert. "You ain't a true Southerner 'less you eat your sweets first. Might have a heart attack, could be a earthquake, and never get to dessert!"

"You're serious – you're eating pie and cake now?" Linda laughed.

"Mama never let me, but Mama's gone, bless her heart."

And then it was time for whiskey and pie, at least for the men, while the women gathered in the kitchen to run the dishwasher and hand wash what wouldn't fit. It was clear that Trish wanted to talk about Ben's situation, but with his boss Larry's wife working the plastic wrap station, she let it go with significant glances as long as she could. At last, though, Laquisha slipped away to the bathroom. Trish nudged Sarah's arm to ask, "Is he takin' this alright?"

Sarah set her dishrag down. "Oh Trisha, I don't know."

"Jared says these things can get to you."

"You wouldn't think, I mean after all he's...."

Trisha touched her arm. "It's a strange crew these spinal cord boys."

"It is."

Then Laquisha returned and they let it drop. Sarah reached in the cupboard and pulled out her secret stash, a box of *Gearhart's* chocolates, and offered them around to the ladies, all in high spirits the way you can get after making yourself useful to the hostess. Linda asked, "Well, it's time, I guess? Let's see how this goes. I'll get Troy to bring it in."

Sarah squared her chin and nodded before turning towards the den.

There's always one, it seems, the girl who doesn't understand the rules and hangs back with the men, throwing back a whiskey and talking sports. It's usually a younger one, and more power to them. This time it was Troy's new girl, the slight blonde thing in the mohair sweater. When Troy came back from the truck he had his guitar with him, a ploy to hide the real reason for his trip outside, and he took a seat on the corner table and tinkered with it. He asked, "Hey Ben, you played since your fall?"

Ben sat with a full tumbler of some too sweet bourbon on ice, a concoction ruined by a candy infusion or something, and shot Troy a surly look. He growled, "How the fuck I'm gonna do that, dude?"

Troy grimaced at his miscue, and let it go. A man's gotta handle bad luck in his own way, he thought, though heaven knows old Ben's had his share. He tuned up a minute, then launched into the usual James Taylor repertoire, his deep and resonant speaking voice somehow transmuted into a nasal whine when he sang. He did "Isn't it Nice to Be Home Again," and "Sweet Baby James" with it's a propos verse about snow on the roads, and he was working his way up to "You've Got a Friend" when his girlfriend sidled up and began to hum along. At that, the guys stopped their chatting. The women were back, crowding the kitchen door, and only the children kept at their games, tapping away on their screens by the tree.

Troy finished his song with a sheepish nod and said, "You wanna try one?" Amy shrugged, "Okay, if you insist," as he was already strumming the intro to a Joni Mitchell tune, that oldie but goodie, "Both Sides Now." Damn, the collective thought arrived, that girl can sing! It wasn't exactly a Joni voice with its loopy range, but she unfurled a sweet and pure soprano that knew when to bend off key, and by the time she was done even the kids had looked up from their corner. All applauded and cheered, but Ben sat stock still as if hypnotized. This girl, how strange, from her first note she'd been channeling his daughter, who had somehow come into the room with them again, 10-year old Caroline sharing a tuneful prayer in the voice of this woman, and wouldn't she be about her age now? He felt a hand at his shoulder. Sarah. The ghost had taken her too.

Or maybe not. There was something else afoot, and everybody seemed to be in on it. "What's this?" he pondered. Sarah took the wheelchair's handles and helped him pivot around towards the front door. There stood Buster, snow dusting the shoulders of his dress grays, leaning over a gleaming red wheelchair. Jared motored over to it, spun back to face the crowd, and offered, "This is for you, Ben, our best and dearest friend, our champion. We all pitched in." He took a sip of whiskey from a long straw that ran back to a tumbler snugged into his arm-rest caddy. "Come over and take a look, man."

Sarah watched Ben's eyes narrow, his mouth purse, at this crucial juncture. She prayed that the peer pressure would win him over, that he couldn't refuse his whole crew. Somehow, clueless bozo that he was, Buster seemed to get that he should wait, give Ben some room. The noisy party went silent as if someone had commanded, "Alexa, Stop" to them all.

Ben knew what this was. He'd never admit it, but he'd scoped it out online himself. Solid frame lightweight with motor assist wheels, and a lever axle so you could drive straight with one hand pushing just one rim. Of course, Jared had ordered it custom, and made damned sure it was red just because. But he knew this was tough, that at a level most of their friends would never understand, it meant a kind of surrender. A ballsy thing for them all to have done. But wait.

Ben hunched at the center of this odd silence like a clock ticking, everyone hoping for a chime. So it came as a crazy relief when he nodded for Troy to push him over, and asked Sarah to get his transfer board, and then he did it himself, though it wasn't pretty, bounced over from one chair to the other, leaving an old and now useless friend behind for this red hot chick with the power assist. He reached under a knee to lift one emaciated leg then the other to fit his feet onto the railing, and once fully situated on his new throne looked up abashed at the cheers of the friends he suddenly wished would just get in their cars and go. Because he had just realized what they could not know. This was the missing piece, the part of the puzzle he had not been able to make fit. But now.

And, of course, there was more to do. The gift swap tradition, everyone bringing some re-wrapped ridiculous item no one would really want or could possibly need from the loot they'd opened the day before, those dime store gimcracks and tchotchkes and gizmos and gadgets that workers in Asia fit together by the millions, then box and crate and ship across wintry seas to end sprinkled in homes across the whole U.S. Insane all the way around! But in some way, this was important, and key to the holiday, too, to be reminded in such a frivolous way how overwhelming is the reach of our empire.

But eventually, yes, they were done. Uncle Al and Aunt Nellie the first to go, laden with leftovers, she protesting, "But we didn't bring a thing! But please, yes, just one little sliver more of that bourbon pecan pie!" Then Jared and Trish gathered their sleepy kids, switched them into onesies in the bathroom and hauled them all down the ramp. On the way out, a toddler draped over his lap, Jared tapped his chair against Ben's, and pleaded, "I know, Ben. I know. Give it a chance?"

Ben bit his lip and nodded. He said, "You'll never know what you mean to me, my friend."

'That's the whiskey talking, brother. It's all about the love, right?"

Ben nodded. "Get them kids home safe now."

"Oh yeah, you know it. Trish hasn't had a swig since before dinner. She's drivin'."

"That a boy."

Then it was Larry and Laquisha, oddly turning at the door in farewell as if scanning this warm and loving home for the last time, Buster and Linda refusing to take more than a single plate of leftovers for tomorrow, and Troy – cheeks red from the cold and exertion of brushing snow off everyone's windshields –

gathering up his guitar and his songbird Amy. She had found Rylie asleep in the guest room, but got her up and out; they'd make sure she got home okay. The Pulliam's, the Stovall's, the Miller's, the Kent's. Good night, y'all; sleep tight; drive safe; it's been great as always; love you all; Happy New Year if we don't see you; good night my dears, good night.

Which left them alone again. Sarah bent to collect the last of the wrapping paper scattered about the tree, and the brisk way she did it said all Ben needed to know about how she'd taken his behavior. Acted the grump. Slammed way too much whiskey. Dumped himself onto the floor and rolled around trying to build Legos with the kids but only freaked them out, spilling his drink on the rug. And it had taken Buster and Troy both to lift him back into his chair and then the cap came off his urine bag and spilled. But the finisher was how he'd begged Amy to sing that Joni song again, and when she obliged he'd started bawling over Caroline, breaking everyone's heart, so they'd pulled out pretty quick after that. Never even bothered to take the tree down. The worst. Pissed as she was, Sarah still dutifully asked if he wanted help getting ready for bed, but he shook his head no, I'll just sit and stare at the lights, you go on, you're tired. And sick of his shit, that's exactly what she'd done.

Well that's that, he fumed, a testy anger welling in his chest. How many times had he told that fucking lie? That since the injury he was a better man. More grateful. More balanced. Aware of life's fragility and its grace. In speeches at high schools and gimp conferences and on Capitol Hill. Parents who'd lost their own kids came up to shake his hand, hoping for the resilience he seemed to radiate. People in wheelchairs lined up like a train to talk camber and gloves and chest straps but really just to rub some of that inspirational energy, that never say die courage, off of him. Some days he even believed what Sarah had said from Day One. It was not your fault, so there's nothing to forgive, but if you need to hear it, I forgive you.

Not a sound in the house, beyond the whisper of the heat pump out back. The tree lights twinkling their tedious semaphor of primary colors. A new and ringing silence from the snow falling outside, that spectral blanketing whine that seems to come from inside your own head. Sarah loved it, she'd wake up in the morning with the field outside a dazzling white and that blanketed loveliness before any wild thing had laid down a track would wipe away any reckoning from the party. She'd put on her new sweater, swap out the plates in the dishwasher and move about the house all day in a busy rapture. Again he'd be forgiven; she'd probably never even mention it.

Suffocating, though, all this sifting snow that could only white out the bedraggled world for a winkling minute. That was fine with her, somehow. She misread the message of the cold front, its enmity, but he felt it to his bones. Perfect to have snow now trapped as they were at the end of a tragic novel dwindling down to its final pages. Where things would get worse and never better until it dawned on her at last that what she had forgiven was unforgivable, her whole life. She would have to do more and more as he did less and less. That was never their agreement, at least not as he understood it. Ben's job was to make it work, to live a wheeled life without a hitch, no surrender to the chair, and that effort was his way to get past it all, and until the fucking arm it had almost worked. He *Open Sesame'd* the front door, the cold swirling in like a spirit from the dark.

The snow came sideways in gusts, so the wind chimes on the back porch sang. He'd recovered the door hook from the corner, exactly where he'd thrown it, pulled his parka around his shoulders and shoved a stocking cap lopsided on his head. The tires of the new wheelchair skidded a little, making tracks down the ramp to the car. A dry snow, whipping, some kind of blast down from Canada they'd said. There would be drifts and busted pipes and no melt for a week at least. Deep freeze cold. At the end of the ramp he wondered if he'd made a mistake, realizing that he'd already gone too far. He could not make it back up to the door alone and half the plan had been leaving his phone on the table.

The damned strap she'd gifted him worked like a charm, hooked onto the door rim. He came in from the passenger side, pulling all his weight up and out of the chair with his good arm, then grabbed the steering wheel and dragged himself across the bench seat like a carcass. He wedged himself against the driver's door, then worked his way up to a seated position one tug at a time, his labored breaths frosting the windshield from inside. He left the chair where it sat. Wouldn't need it. But then, no. He had to pull it in or they'd figure it out. Damn. So he let himself topple sideways across the seat, onto his bad arm, and reaching far overhead skittered the chair closer on the ice, popped off one wheel, and tossed it with a clattering heave behind him on the rear seat. He lay there trying to catch his breath from that effort, snot freezing in his nostrils. Every squirrel in the county high in a tree bole wrapped in its fluffy tail.

Why not just stop? This would be fine, this could work. But the jab of lying on his ruined shoulder woke him to his task. It took a long time. The first thing you learn is that everything takes a long time. Then, lesson two, so what else were you going to do? The wheelless chair finally propped beside him on the seat, he figured the passenger door would swing shut once he got going. But he was ready now and had to trust that Sarah was truly out, would not hear the engine catch from her room in back.

Ben hadn't tried it yet, but why not, the old hand controls, you could manipulate them with one hand, you just had to be smart, play it safe, it could work. The scribbled note: *Went to get eggs and bacon.* The *Walmart* at the Mall along the way would be the only thing open this late. It all made a sort of sense. It was just like him, tipsy, to think about a breakfast surprise for the hostess to thank her for all she'd done for everybody the night before. A way to make up for his bad behavior.

A flat skim of trackless road lay bright in his headlights, snow ghosts striding from tree line to tree line. He knew exactly where to veer, had rehearsed this in his passing for years. Only two short miles from the safety of home, they'd almost made it around this last curve. A sleepover night on a tournament weekend in a time that sang like heaven. The skid swung the heavy sedan's rear with the satisfying whip of a carnival ride backwards down the embankment, wheels squealing for a grip, then that thing he'd tried so hard to remember, the abrupt abutment of a tree trunk that this time, wouldn't you know it, only broke his nose on the wheel.

Through the cracked windshield, he watched as a ring of skeletal trees woke at this affront and shook their naked limbs. Snow spilled from their boughs like shaken sand. Then they pulled themselves up by their roots, men tugging heavy boots from sucking mud, before clasping each others' outstretched branches like spectral hands, proceeding to march or maybe they were trying to dance in a circle around the car. It was a welcoming sort of trudge, though impossibly surreal, as if they sought to communicate, what comes next may be horrible or wonderful, get ready.

The driver side door tilted downhill and opened with the touch of an elbow. He allowed himself to tip sideways onto a virgin drift then used that same trusty elbow to nudge along, he had all night after all, to the exact spot he sought. He stretched out flat there, gasping. Then remembered the flask of vodka in his vest pocket and tugged it out, twisting the top off with his teeth. The trees now began to sway as if waltzing. The snow from their shaking dusted his coat, his useless legs, his splayed nose. If horrible things led to a wonderful reunion, then let's get on with it, he thought, lifting his head to take a long draught with a bite but no flavor, as if distilled from snow. Then he lay back, outstretched at the threshold of some new place, where no one played tennis or needed catheters, and he prayed that it looked enough like an accident so the insurance would pay out.

Sarah would be angry at first, devastated. Such a heartless thing to do. But eventually she'd notice that her burden had shifted, slipped off her shoulders, she would walk with a lighter step and the creases in her brow would smooth. She would take down the ramp, unbolt the grab rails from the bathroom walls, she would meet a man who could dance and stroll hand in hand along a river path. Ben's nose bled salty into his mouth. He took another long swig to wash out the taste. There was nothing to do but settle in the cushioning drift, the way he had as a boy making snow angels. He lifted his eyes to the dancing trees, licked out to catch a snowflake on his tongue.

Billy. His son. What will he think? How will it distort that oddly heroic image he's always had of his gimp dad? Well, that needed to die. A lie through and through. There was a letter, but he hoped now that they'd never find it. He'd tucked it away in an old baseball jacket in Billy's closet, imagining it would be one of the last things Sarah would get to in her eventual cleaning house. So useless, he saw now, any effort to explain. But he did want them to understand one thing, long after the money paid out. It was only honest to admit his intent. This was no accident. As mean as it was, as much as it had to hurt everyone he loved and cared for, he needed them to be sure of that. Jared, Troy, all the old friends, he was just their personal charity, it made them feel good to care. But Sarah, for all the road she'd traveled, how could she ever forgive?

My God, how long a life is! But there you go again, this was

Ben's great fault, his infernal sentimentality, always sawing at that phantom violin. It had made him want to set everything aright. It had driven him to try and fix the world. But that was not possible, the world was irrevocably broken, snapped at the spine and dangling, though skulking ichor yet pulsed to its purple toes. So that's why I've done it, he thought. These plodding trees mere sentiment, the imaginings of a sodden drunk. There can be no reunion, and no redo, no coming back for more. This was no time for fairy tales, though the ancient trees danced and their limbs soughed in the wind. The old Joni Mitchell song echoed again, an ear worm, tra la-ing both sides now, and his eyes cut to one side as if glimpsing her up on a limb. A thin smile formed on his icy lips, ah frail Joni with your long blonde hair and narrow shoulders, come with me to this other side, let's write a fourth verse to go along with your themes of clouds and love and life.

She may not be there, that seemed to be what the plodding trees were teasing, you have made another mistake. As always, you wayward fool. But it was not his mistake. That had been made by the trees themselves all those years ago. They took the wrong ones, or left their work incomplete. As the chipped white oak, the oldest of the copse, made its round, he reached for the faded pink ribbon waving at its waist. If he could touch it, even if it was the last thing he ever did, perhaps it would also be the first. Oh rest. Oh let it be. He glimpsed blue lights bobbing in the woods, and hoped they were rescuers, because even now the half of his body that worked reconsidered, thought to go back and face the music again. But the other half prayed that it was too late. Maybe the blue lights marked the next phase in the dance, where he like the trees might stand and shake a leg. Where he might finally give up the weight of reckoning that had made an existence – he wouldn't call it a life – more hellish on its best day than whatever yet might come.

GRANDPA AND THE BEAR

We stood there in ankle deep snow, my mom and I, the door tugged open and our jaws slack, having followed my Grandpa's boot tracks to the shed in the woods where he lay snoring, cuddled close to the furry back of a monstrous black bear. It's gone viral now, thanks to my brother posting the video on Instagram. Grandpa on *The Today Show* and *ellen*, the bear, we all hope, safely off tromping the woods. But in the family, when we discuss it, we try to go back to that first moment, not when we found them, but way before, back when this whole thing started.

It's Grandma dying. You're familiar with that part from your own experience; is there a family in America that doesn't know cancer? The happy camper who develops an odd cough or a twinge, and then the grim diagnosis with its confusing prognostic window. The promising treatments, the temporary remission, opportunities to get together with family one more, maybe two more times, the scarves and wigs, the winnowing. The bedside vigils and the tears and the way cellular rebellion comes on slow enough for hope, but then awfully fast. That's where it started for us, Grandma's decade-long bout with lymphoma eventually mutating into other eventually untreatable invasions. She was young, we say, when it came on. Mid-50s, early retired from an office manager's position, a weekly tennis player and Sunday School teacher, a gardener and cook. She was very old, though just 65, when her head turned slowly towards us from the reclined Barcalounger in her den to the kitchen where we nibbled our breakfast and took her last shallow breath.

Grandma had expected it to go this way. It was a consideration of her second marriage, when she wed a man a decade younger. He would probably outlive her. Grandpa, though, poo poo'ed such a worry. They would live forever. And even when she took sick, he trusted that there was always one more treatment, one more diet, one more protocol that would keep her chugging along. But as we know, that works until it doesn't.

Grandpa came home from the funeral to the suddenly enormous and empty four-bedroom, two story with full basement frame house they'd built and lived in for the twenty years of their marriage, and set about the highly individualized and unshareable derangement that is the mourning of a spouse. We live in Virginia, far from the wooded Highlands of New Jersey, so we took our own mourning home with us, and learned of Grandpa's travails mostly in nightly tearful phone calls to Mom. We first visited again a month later and learned firsthand how things had changed.

Grandpa is not related to us, as they say, by blood. Mom's father and her mom divorced when she was a teenager; both remarried happily, and until Grandma's demise, had remained so. But being a younger guy, not much older than our dad, Grandpa made a rousing playmate in our youth. He's the Grandpa who bought us a go-cart; who fired solid fuel rockets with toy parachutes; who carved snow chutes for our sleds down the long slope of his yard into the woods. He's a salesman, makes a good living that way, but Mom has always said he's just a kid at heart. Which, I suppose, could help explain the whole thing with the bear.

We drove up the Jersey Turnpike and veered off on the Garden State Parkway, eventually wending our way into the mountains alongside rushing trout streams and all the summer cottages that dot glacier moraine lakes in that part of the world. We saw deer, a raccoon, almost struck an opossum nibbling garbage on the roadside. People think of New Jersey as a stinking industrial hell, but if you get up north where the Appalachian Trail passes through, it's as pretty as any place in the East. But for Grandpa, with Grandma gone, all that solitude made its own sort of hell.

Our first indication that things had changed came in the kitchen. They'd remodeled it twice since moving in, always opting for more features, more cabinets, more conveniences. Grandma kept her kitchen shipshape, and left a sparkling marble and cherry galley with two convection ovens and two microwaves, a gas-fired restaurant stove, a pair of dishwashers located either side of a sink you could bathe a Labrador retriever in, and every gadget from flip waffle irons to instant pots, all neatly tucked away in acres of cabinets, the doors of which closed with a whisper. An inveterate bargain shopper, she had packed every free space with enough food to support a summer camp. All to feed two old folks, neither of whom ate all that much, and to cook the one holiday meal Grandma managed each year, our annual Christmas Eve Feast of Seven Fishes, when all the Italian kids, grandkids, aunts and uncles on Mom's side descended. It was overkill, yes, but people with means do kitchens like that these days, whether they need them or not. Grandpa, whose experience of cooking was all on the outdoor grill, certainly had no need.

So when we arrived, it surprised us to see the cabinets above the left-hand dishwasher gaping open without doors. Mom

immediately asked about it, even before we'd stowed our suit-
cases upstairs, and Grandpa – standing unshaven before us in
pajamas and slippers he'd clearly worn all day – explained that
he had sent the doors out for refinishing. You see, he explained,
he came back from the funeral that awful afternoon and
standing sobbing at the sink with a full glass of whiskey in his
hand, his reflection distorted and ghostly in the darkened
window, he'd noticed a smudge of some sort on the cabinet door
nearest the sink. Probably one of us, a funeral visitor, had acci-
dentally besmirched Grandma's kitchen in this way.

Grandpa put down the glass of whiskey, blew his nose, and
went to work, first with a sponge and dishwashing liquid, then
with a Brillo pad and a solvent he kept in the garage. He found
other smudges, and another on the adjoining cabinet door. On
his first night alone he found a way to stay occupied. At three he
fell asleep in the same Barcalounger where Grandma had
breathed her last just days before; he said it still smelled of her
perfume. When he awoke the next morning, he realized that he
had scrubbed the finish off the cabinet doors entirely, so the
wood seemed leopard spotted, all but ruined. That couldn't
stand.

Grandpa told us all of this in a rambling not quite on point
style that probably derived from his salesman's pitch, extraneous
details flecked in to disguise and deflect, but his eyes flickered,
held a wildness, that made it seem he was playing both
salesman and mark in this scenario, working hard to close the
deal but not quite buying it either. He phoned the guy who'd
built the cabinets, complained of shoddy workmanship, and
ordered him to take the doors to his shop to refinish them as
best he could. It won't be easy, Grandpa said; he needs to match
the finish elsewhere, and that will be a challenge. But it's what,
he concluded – and here is the line that made the sale –
Grandma would have wanted.

The next morning, our dad made a huge mistake. Our whole lives, on weekend mornings, he's dragged himself out of bed early to make us bacon and waffles. It's what he'll be remembered for at his funeral one day. Worrying that Grandpa hadn't been eating well, he pulled out Grandma's flip waffler as quietly as he could, found the requisite bowls and spoons and multigrain flours (he'd brought buttermilk, maple syrup and his secret ingredient – a cup of applesauce – from home), and by the time we all got up Grandpa's house smelled as fragrant as an IHOP or Denny's, bacon strips plaited across a grate with paper towels underneath, and a platter stacked high with Belgian-style waffles waiting on the kitchen's marble-topped island.

Dad had wiped off the waffle iron, dabbed up drips of batter, but otherwise left it sitting on the kitchen counter to cool before putting it away. He knew, he recalled on the ride home, what a stickler Grandpa could be about cleanliness, about keeping things in order – after all, a funny story from our childhoods was how Grandpa had gone to work repainting the hallway baseboards even as we were packing to leave after a Christmas visit, when my three year old brother had bumped them with his new Big Wheels trike. So we might have expected this problem. But Grandpa came down, looked furtively about the fragrant kitchen, opened the dishwasher now stacked with mixing bowls, then spurned the chunky waffles for jelly on toast and a coffee. Something was up. And then he couldn't hold back any longer. We call it the "Waffle Iron Episode" now.

Grandpa got up and walked over to my Dad, who sat oblivious, happily tapping his iPad at the kitchen table with a last drop of syrup on his mustache, and lit into him. He used the phrase, "How dare you?" He waved his hands in dismay, slapped one open palm down on the table, his face had gone purple as we'd never seen it before. Dad sat calmly at the table, maybe leaning back in his chair a little, with an expression on his face of anthropological wonder. So this is how it looks, he seemed to be thinking. And then he spoke, with the extra calmness we know well from our own transgressions over the years, using a voice calibrated down to chill the situation, while also nailing it to the wall: "I'm sorry, I didn't think, I understand, yes, you can be sure, I will not use your waffle iron again."

We ate out the rest of that trip. Mom and Dad sat with Grandpa in the living room before we left and attempted the magic trick of asking him to see a counselor, maybe consider an anti-depressant, come visit. Grandpa got up and retrieved a broom to sweep the kitchen for the tenth time that day. He thanked us for being concerned, but we all knew they hadn't reached him. He still seemed bothered by the waffle iron episode. He'd spent nearly an hour cleaning its little tefloned metal indentations before wrapping it in cellophane, returning it to the box it came in, and replacing it in the cabinet where it belonged. His eyes searched for crumbs, though to us the kitchen, indeed the whole house, seemed spotless as a museum.

Back home, Grandpa's calls adopted a new theme. At dinner, Mom recounted how he'd grill her about Grandma's everyday routines. What days did she shop? What website did she use for store coupons? When did she wash whites and on what setting? Did she vacuum every other day or weekly? In the freezer, did she have a system for rotating meats? Mom said she tried to tell him that none of this mattered any more, that it was up to him now to establish his own routines, but apparently that was the last thing he wanted to hear, so he took his worried questions to Aunt Marie instead. Then Mom and her sister ended up on the phone after dinner, counseling each other about how to help Grandpa get over this hump.

A few weeks later a Nor'easter plowed up the Delaware River, bulldozing trees and knocking out power all across north Jersey. Our dad was able to get through on Grandpa's cellphone and asked how things were going. Grandpa said he was stuck at home, that the roads in to work were blocked with lines down everywhere, and it looked like the electricity grid would be out for days. Dad remembered that Grandpa had a gasoline-powered generator and asked if he'd set it up. Grandpa said something like, "Yeah, it's running pretty good, but I had to make a choice. Either keep the power on for the freezer and the fridge or feed the A.C. upstairs here in the bedroom. It's pretty stuffy up here, but I can't sleep anyway, so whatever."

Dad asked him what was in the freezer that was so important, and that set Grandpa off on an indignant rant (so Dad said) about the steaks and pork roasts Grandma had stacked there, but most importantly about the tins of home-made Christmas cookies, each tiny snowball shaped and rolled in powdered sugar by Grandma's living hands. Grandpa's main gripe, however, was that with the trees down he couldn't make the eight mile drive out past the reservoir to the mausoleum by a Catholic chapel in the woods where we'd buried Grandma. He said, yes, he was still visiting her before and after work, then went on to describe how he would stand with his hands on the smooth granite face of the crypt, one on the sealed door that held Grandma's coffin, the other on the adjoining crypt that would one day hold his, and sometimes, he said, tears actually pooled on the stone floor at his feet. He was crying as he said this, Dad recalled. He said, "It should have been me. She doesn't belong there. She was so good. She was perfect, always." Dad told us all this at dinner. He added, "It's been months. Old Christmas cookies? Perfect? I mean, seriously?"

We drove up before school started in August, and that's when our folks really got concerned. For one thing, this time all the cabinet doors in the kitchen were gone. Grandpa said the guy couldn't match the finish like he wanted, so he'd ordered the whole bank redone. It was weird to stand in Grandma's showroom galley with all the cabinets open, her endless stacks of dried foods and teas and spices and condiments displayed as if on store shelves. I made a mistake that caused Grandpa to jump, moving a stack of mail to set down my laptop on the kitchen table. He said, "Sit somewhere else, will you? That's where Grandma left her mail, and I don't want you rearranging things."

It was the same everywhere. On the one hand, the strange disorder with the missing cabinet doors, on the other hand an obsessive focus on keeping things exactly as they were on that day back in the Spring when Grandma died. Mom had made an overture about maybe cleaning out the clothes closets and Grandpa initially agreed, then balked when she bent to Grandma's shoe racks and ordered her out of their bedroom suite. On the way out, she noticed a rolled up sleeping bag next to the bed with a pillow stacked atop it. The California King that nearly fills the room was neatly made up, Grandma's Mickey and Minnie Mouse dolls leaning against the headboard holding hands. Was Grandpa sleeping on the floor? That was a question nobody dared to ask. Mom said Grandma's wigs still sat displayed on tripods in a row along the bureau top, the bureau itself, like all the other horizontal surfaces around the house, thick with dust. Again, our parents sat with Grandpa before we left, and it seemed as if nothing had changed. He had tried a therapy group, but felt the other widows and widowers there were pathetic. He disdained the idea of anti-depressants, explaining, "Look, I have a damned good reason to be upset, depressed if you want to call it, this isn't some chemical imbalance you straighten out with a pill."

Mom told him, "Don't you see, we're all mourning. She was my mother," but Grandpa wouldn't hear it. He said, "I lost my mother, too, but it wasn't like this, you just don't know."

One cool thing happened that trip, though. I went out for a run early the second day before things got too hot and noticed that all the garbage cans along the street were overturned with trash strewn everywhere. At first I blamed some high schooler with a grudge, but then stopped dead in my tracks on a curve face-to-face with a shaggy black bear, who on his hind legs hugging a garbage can stood taller than me. He lifted his head from the can to give me a quizzical look, a piece of wrapping paper stuck like a dinner napkin to his chin. He tipped the can over, sniffed at its treasures a moment, then trundled off across the neighbor's yard back into the woods, thus ending his dawn rampage and my run. I noticed that he favored his right front leg, barely setting it down. It made him seem human, somehow. Back at the house, I expected Grandpa to blow up, what with trash scattered across his yard, but instead he just pulled on a pair of jeans and old sneaks, and joined me in raking up the mess. He said, "Yeah, that's old Tripod, we call him. He got hit by a car back last Fall, just down the road near the post office, and must have broken his leg."

Grandpa said the police in the next town over had shot a bear recently for no good reason. Developers run homes right up the mountain face now, he said, and apparently some lady had built a pool in her backyard atop the bear's hibernation cave. When the old bear returned for a good winter's nap, her cave was gone, and in its place strained a yappy Pomeranian leashed to a pool chair. The lady said it only took the bear one swipe to send the pup sailing into the pool, dead on splashdown. The bear then nestled in a stack of pool noodles beside a gazebo and fell asleep. They didn't have to shoot her; they could have just tranquilized her and hauled her further into the Highlands, but the lady had connections, was furious, and the expense and all. Killed the bear right where she lay, causing a shit storm of anger from all the local tree huggers. Sheriff, Grandpa added, might even lose his job over it.

"Old Tripod," Grandpa said, "He's pushing his luck, too. You did the right thing to come home. Bears are unpredictable on a good day, and he's wounded, so that's worse. I keep a shotgun in the garage now, you never know."

So I wasn't really surprised when we got a call during breakfast one day after school started, Grandpa frantic, bereft, almost unable to express his dismay at what a bear had done. He'd made the mistake of leaving the garage door open after one last lawn mowing of the season, had wanted the riding mower to cool off half-way in the door, and that had been all the invitation needed. A bear had moseyed into the garage during the night, deftly opened the freezer door, and completely demolished all the carefully labeled food stacked there. But the worst of it, he'd gotten into Grandma's cookies, smashed the tin when he couldn't get the lid off, and dragged it out to the yard. Nothing left but crumbs of her sweetest legacy, her precious lovingly hand-made treats. We all sat there holding our cereal spoons, Grandpa on speakerphone, imagining him in his pajamas on his knees in the front yard, tearfully collecting crumbs in a dented tin.

Mom invited Grandpa down for Thanksgiving, but he begged off. Dad gave this sort of benedictory prayer about the spirits of those who have gone on watching over us, and Mom teared up. It was weird having more room at the dining table. Aunt Marie half-joked about Grandpa not wanting to be away from Grandma too long, and Dad said he'd read somewhere about how holidays can be the worst, that they signify time passing, which sucks. Grandpa had long ago stopped his nightly check-ins, didn't say much when he did call, didn't seem interested in our soccer seasons or anything. A week or so later, Mom phoned to see if he would maybe participate in our Christmas grab-bag again, but she couldn't get through. She looked up the company where Grandpa works and they said he hadn't checked in for a few days, but not to worry. He'd been known to wander off the reservation on occasion, always returning with new clients and commissions.

But Mom did worry. She postponed our usual weekend for putting up the Christmas tree and let me leave school early on Friday, so we could take turns on the long drive "over the river and through the woods" to check on him. She called Grandpa every hour on the drive, but nothing. By Exit 8 on the Turnpike you could see crusty snow on the shoulder, and I had to turn on the wipers when new snow started to fall pretty heavily on the Parkway. But we made the drive in the usual seven hours, pulling into Grandpa's neighborhood just after dark. It was odd to see his driveway unswept. One of Grandpa's many gadgets is a snow blower attachment for his riding mower, and he had always been religious about keeping the pavement clean.

The house was dark, but Mom knows the garage door combination – Grandma and Grandpa's wedding day – so we let ourselves in that way. We crept through the house, turning on lights, calling out, both of us a little creeped out and afraid of what we might find. The place looked exactly as always, except the kitchen cabinet doors had all been rehung. That made the house seem even more like a time capsule or something. Grandma's wigs still sat propped on their tripods, and the Minnie and Mickey Mouse dolls leaned together on the bed exactly as she remembered them, their wide black eyes staring up at a corner of the ceiling. On the kitchen table, I noticed that same stack of bills Grandpa had warned me not to move. But the refrigerator was all but empty, just a butter dish and a box of baking soda; the freezer in the garage had been unplugged.

Where was he? Mom stood in one spot in the kitchen, revolving slowly to take it all in. She phoned Dad and used the word "shrine." She said, "It's like nothing has changed since she died. Except the freezer, and that Christmas cactus she doted on? It's dead." We decided to order a pizza and give ourselves a moment to collect our thoughts. They said with the snow it would take a while, so I pulled on a pair of Grandpa's galoshes and went outside to get my wiggles out from the long drive. Cold wind rattled the treetops, sweeping snow across the hills. It was like there was this high almost-perceptible dog whistle in the air, and the cottony new snow gave to a crunch of ice underneath. It was that wisp of frontier I liked to make believe was still alive on my childhood romps in the woods.

I was thinking about that as I walked down the side-yard hill where Grandpa carved our sled runs. Then I noticed an imprint of boot tracks, almost dusted over, leading down to the plywood shed he'd let us use as a fort back in the day. He'd kept it up, even kept it painted, he was that guy. I leaned in at the garage door and asked Mom to come out. I didn't want to go down there by myself. So together we found him, and the bear.

Everybody seems to think it's funny now. I do, sort of. But Mom and I know better. We remember pretty well the shock of it, the two of them lying spooned together, the bear curled into himself, nose buried in his haunch, Grandpa making a C-shape around the curve of his back and his arm in its coat and mittens outstretched familiarly across the hairy beast. Together they pretty much filled the shed floor, both of them snoring, our phone flashlights playing across the scene. That's what you see in the video. Why I did that I'll never know. I just couldn't process it, it was a reflex or something. And then when my brother put it up on Instagram.

Maybe what we did was nuts, but then the whole thing lay outside our comfort zone. Mom and I were afraid to touch him or to say anything; we didn't want to wake up the bear. Grandpa's snoring proved he was okay, we whispered, so we just eased the door closed and left them there. We went in the house, called Dad and Aunt Marie, and I texted my brother and this girl I know, and we just went to bed. Mom said Grandpa looked like he was getting the best sleep he'd had all year. Which I guess made us feel a little better about leaving him out there in the cold. I lay in my guest room bed all night, unable to sleep, with – yep – an old teddy bear in the crook of my arm. But I must have drifted off, because the next thing I knew there was Grandpa sitting at the foot of the bed, still in his coat and stocking cap, bright sunlight pouring in the window.

Grandpa said, "So you saw, huh? I noticed your footsteps in the snow."

I pushed the teddy bear aside and reached out for his arm. I said, "Grandpa."

"Yeah. I know. Look. I'm gonna need your help explaining this to your mom."

I waited. He said, "It's old Tripod."

I nodded.

"I think he's the guy who broke into the freezer. Anyway, he's been coming around. I got home from work one day and he'd been pawing at the garage door. You can still see the scratches, haven't had time to paint them over, but I will.

"Anyway," Grandpa said, "I guess it was a couple weeks ago, I found one last tin of cookies in the basement fridge. Was gonna save them for Christmas, surprise everybody, like one last gift she'd left us or something. But I didn't do that."

I said, "Okay."

Grandpa took off his stocking cap and scratched his head. His hair was longer than I'd ever seen it, straggly and streaked with gray. It was the first time he'd ever looked like an old man to me. I think tears came into my eyes. He said, "What I did instead. It wasn't like I was thinking or anything. It was like so much of everything ever since. I was being a robot or something. But I left a cookie out on the back step. And the next day another one. And old Tripod, he was a gentleman about the whole thing. I'd just pour a cup of coffee and wait by the door, and he'd come doddering up from the creek, and snuffle it up. He knew I was there. He'd lift his head to sniff the air like he was nodding along to some music only bears can hear, and it was like we made eye contact or something."

I said, "Yeah, he sorta did that the day I saw him."

"Yeah, right. And you know how he limps along holding that front paw up?"

I smiled, remembering.

Grandpa dropped his hand to my foot; it was cold, but I didn't pull away. He continued, "It was after our first snow, right around Thanksgiving, when everybody wanted me to come down. I couldn't get out to see Grandma, the power went out for a day or so, and when I went to leave his cookie, I noticed his tracks. He'd gotten into your fort, had nuzzled the door open somehow, and he was kneeling there kind of groggy like he was ready to nod off and hibernate on the spot. It was just like you found us. He didn't mind me being there. I put a cookie down by his paw, and this long tongue like you wouldn't believe whipped it up, and left a lick of powdered sugar on his muzzle. And then he licked that, too. Then he closed his eyes with this, it was almost like a blissful smile, if bears can even do that."

I nodded, completely seeing what he was saying.

"And that's when I did it, what you saw. This is what I need your help with. I don't know if your mom will understand. But you met him before, so maybe. The thing is, they try, they really do. But people don't get it. They don't know. I mean, this house. But old Tripod. Do you see?"

I'm seventeen. I don't do this much anymore. But I scrunched up closer and reached my arm around for a hug. I had no idea what he was talking about, but you do what you have to do.

On tv, Grandpa told Ellen pretty much the same thing. For a salesman, he's not the most articulate person in the world. Or maybe it's just the deep stuff that can be hard to get to, I don't know. It didn't matter, though. Because what he discovered is that people do get it. They knew exactly what he was saying about what he had done. He got so many letters from so many people who have holes in their hearts that cannot be filled. And maybe it helped.

It's summer as I write this. I'm lying on a ridgetop in my sleeping bag, while Grandpa snores beside me. We're off exploring the Highlands for a week or so, not even really following any kind of trail. He's put the house up for sale, looking for a smaller place, maybe one of those vacation cabins off the road along a trout stream, but still not too far from the mausoleum. With the sale and the money from the talk shows, he figures he can retire. Says he wants to go off the grid. Has some things he wants to figure out. I get that. But what he's really doing, he's looking for old Tripod. He's got a cookie in his backpack for his old pal, the one solitary guy who knows how to play this game.

ABOUT THE AUTHOR

Tony Gentry is the author of a novel *The Coal Tower* and five young adult biographies. He has worked as a security guard, jazz club busboy, art museum preparator, French Quarter waiter, radio news producer, late night legal proofreader and word processor, occupational therapist, and professor, and has sojourned in Boston, New Orleans, New York, Hoboken, Los Angeles, Fort Wayne, and Raleigh before straggling back to his home environs in central Virginia. He now works at Virginia Commonwealth University, four blocks from the hospital where he was born.

Tony holds degrees from Harvard College (BA), New York University (MA), and The University of Virginia (PhD). He lives in Bon Air, Virginia, with his wife Christine, also an occupational therapist, their two sons and their dog Buddy. He keeps a prose and verse blog at tonygentry.com.